RUNNERS

ALSO BY PHIL OAKLEY

Little Hatchet (Book One of The Oakleys)

The Morello Family: Pin Raids

The Morello Family: War

The Morello Family: Wave of Carnage

San Juan Bautista

Searching for Moses

RUNNERS

THE OAKLEYS
BOOK 2

PHIL OAKLEY

Published by
Stoney Creek Publishing Group
StoneyCreekPublishing.com

Copyright © 2015 and 2025 by Phil Oakley. All rights reserved.

ISBN: 978-1-965766-14-9
ISBN (ebook): 978-1-965766-15-6
Library of Congress Control Number: 2025901057

No part of this publication may be reproduced, distributed, or transmitted in any form or by any means, including photocopying, recording, or other electronic or mechanical methods, without the prior written permission of the publisher, except in the case of brief quotations embodied in critical reviews and certain other noncommercial uses permitted by copyright law.

Cover design by Market Your Industry, marketyourindustry.com

Originally published in 2015. © *2015 by Phil Oakley*

For my wife Nancy
My Inspiration and My Light for over Fifty Years

Part One
RAY'S RECKLESS ODYSSEYS

CHAPTER ONE

There's not much fall in Telegraph, Texas. The heat and dust don't give up easily. But when September came, five-year-old Ray Oakley tagged along with his brother Brooks for the first day of school. Ray, thirteen months younger than Brooks, wasn't old enough to start school, but the amused teacher agreed to let him try first grade almost two years early.

That's the way Ray was—restless and in a hurry. He couldn't stand to wait, and Ray could never admit that Brooks, or anyone else, could do something better than he could. Better to let him get engaged in school, the teacher reasoned, lest he wind up like his older brothers.

Glenn was dead, and Ralph was who knows where. The rumors around town were that he was running liquor in Louisiana. And then there were the sisters, who already seemed headed for trouble. Everyone in town knew the Oakleys, and out of respect for Walter and Ada, no one spoke openly of how the children had gone astray. The teacher could only imagine the heartbreak that Ada had endured. So if young Ray wanted to come to school a year early, she was happy to help him find the straight and narrow.

But the youngest Oakley brother also became bored quickly. After three days tagging along with Brooks to first grade, Ray announced that school was boring, and he didn't want to go anymore. No one objected. Competing in sports, whether on the schoolyard or anywhere else, was another matter altogether.

For years, the two Oakley boys played with a beat-up old football on the rocky ground in Telegraph. The loose, and not so loose, limestone surface was veined with traces of black dirt. But there was no denying that their games took place on a brutal field of play. Conditions like the ones the Oakleys grew up with along the South Llano River, those things were just normal aspects of Hill Country football. Teeth were knocked out. And several times, Walter, their father, had to take one or both boys to Junction to have gashes to their heads sewn up by the doctor. Nearly always, the cause of injury would be falling on a rocky playing surface. But the bruises, cuts, and knocks never dimmed Brooks' dream. He was absolutely determined to run the football for the University of Texas Longhorns. The name Brooks Oakley was going to be in record books in Austin, no matter what it took, or how much he had to sacrifice.

When Ray restarted his education the next year, every hour spent in a classroom seemed like it would drag on forever. School was so boring. But as soon as the last bell rang, the boys flocked to the school playground, where the endless football games lasted until it was too dark to see the ball. There was never enough time for football. That part of the Oakley brothers' life seemed to have zipped past at the speed of light; and in a flash, Brooks would become a high school running back sensation, turning heads across the state of Texas. It was a full school year before Ray could claim his spot on the roster of the Junction Eagles. Ray was on top of the world in high school so long as he was playing football. But when the season was over and the holidays were past, Ray gave in to boredom.

It was oppressing tedium that compelled Ray to boost himself into an empty box car on a Southern Pacific freight train parked on a siding in Junction. That freight would take Ray east to San Antonio, where he planned to catch a northbound MK&T freight train to Temple. From there he would sneak onto a Santa Fe freight train headed west to California.

CHAPTER TWO

Ray had read in a *Saturday Evening Post* story about railroad security guards beating up people caught riding on freight trains, but he had shoved that information far back into his memory—at least until his train approached the giant Southern Pacific freight yard in San Antonio. Hearing boots pounding on the roof of the boxcar he was riding in brought the information front and center in Ray's mind. He was simultaneously alarmed by screaming both above and around him.

Ray peeked through the cracked door of the boxcar and saw terrified men bolting from the train. A few seconds later, Ray heard an explosion of violent profanity followed by the terrified cries of a man begging not to be hit. Looking out even more cautiously a second time, Ray spotted another horrified man on the ground directly in front of the car Ray was in. Two much larger men were pummeling the hapless transient with ax handles. Ray stole a glance out of the other side of the boxcar. The train was creeping past a string of tank cars parked on an adjacent siding. Concluding that the parked freight cars might provide a safer shelter, Ray leapt from the boxcar, fell to the ground and rolled underneath one of those cars. Ray had fled just in time. Seconds after he had bailed out of the moving train, two men holding ax handles burst into the car Ray had just vacated, storming through the same door Ray had witnessed the beating from. They took a quick look inside, then closed and barred both doors of the freight car.

Ray was getting his first inkling that his idea of a journey through history might be knottier than he had imagined. Ray had been in the railyard for several minutes. He peered out from under the tank car to make sure the bulls had moved on. With no obvious danger in view, Ray crawled out from beneath the car on the side away from the train he had ridden into San Antonio. He stood, straightened his clothes and strode directly out of the railyard. He had been walking on the street for only a moment when he heard someone calling to him.

"Hold it right there!" the voice commanded.

Ray stopped and turned to see a police officer approaching on foot. "Didn't you hear me talking to you?" the cop barked.

"No," Ray shot back. He didn't tolerate being spoken to rudely. Living in a sparsely populated rural county, Ray had never encountered an officer of the law he didn't know, nor one who didn't know Ray, his family, and the Oakleys' place in the community. This was only Ray's second time in San Antonio.

"Don't sass me son, or I'll box your ears," the policeman snarled. "Why aren't you in school?"

Ray rapidly considered a list of potential lies. "I wanted to ride a freight train," he answered honestly after a long pause, the belligerence gone from his voice.

"You can get yourself killed doing that," the officer warned. After a long pause, the officer finally asked, "Where are you going?"

"California," Ray responded.

"But you just came in from the west?" the policeman posed suspiciously.

"Yes sir," Ray said. "But I want to ride the Santa Fe out there, and I have to go to Temple to catch it," the young adventurer explained.

"Come on," the policeman directed, motioning for Ray to get into the police car.

"Am I being arrested?" Ray asked, fearing he was becoming involved in a humiliating situation.

"No, but I'm going to take you someplace where you can catch the Katy without getting your head split open," the officer asserted. Ray rode right through downtown San Antonio in the police car, then up the Austin Highway for several miles north of the city. The policeman pulled over to the side of the road.

"If you're going to ride these trains, you've got to stay out of the freight yards. The railroad bulls will kill you," the officer warned bluntly. "Going through Austin, you should be all right. But watch out when you get to Temple. That's a big junction, and there'll be lots of security there. Any time you come to a big city, jump off before you get into the yard and walk through town. If you don't, you're going to get yourself killed. Most of the bulls carry guns, and some of 'em will shoot you, ride you out into the country, then throw your body off the train. Do you understand?" the sympathetic policeman asked.

"Yes sir," Ray answered appreciatively, openly unnerved by the warning.

"Son, if you have any sense at all, you'll give this up and go home," the officer advised. Ray sat for a time, staring at the dashboard in the police car, his mouth dry and speechless. "How about it?" the cop offered kindly. "Can I put you on a train for home?" Ray sat mute. "I didn't think so," the officer said after waiting for almost a full minute. "But remember what I told you. Most of these guys will kill you quicker than look at you. They're not nice people." The policeman pointed across the road. "There's a big bend between those two rises there," he instructed. And there's the beginning of a long grade rising up starting in the bend. The trains move through that cut very slowly. You can jump on without any problem. Good luck, son" the policeman concluded.

"Thanks," Ray answered as he stepped out of the car. The first train Ray saw was pulled by a Missouri Pacific locomotive. Confused, he started to leap on board but held back at the last second. Ray's plan was to ride a Katy train north to Temple. Three other Missouri Pacific freights passed: two headed into San Antonio and another northbound. Ray was frustrated and wondered whether he was in the right place. He made up his mind to grab the next northbound train, even if it was not the Katy. The early dark of midwinter was descending.

CHAPTER THREE

The Great Depression did not destroy the lives of people around Telegraph to the tragic degree that the economic catastrophe of the 1930s decimated other parts of Texas. Hill Country folks had been too poor before the Depression for it to make that much of a difference. Their farms hadn't been worth enough to mortgage even before the crash of 1929 and most of the farmland in the central Texas hills was so rocky that cash crops were rare.

In much of the rest of Texas—just as in Oklahoma, parts of Arkansas and much of the Midwest—tens of thousands of farm families were being driven off their land every month. The Great Depression was a tragedy so vast that it all but shattered what the world thought of as the American Dream. The Depression was a momentous time, and Ray had a sense of history. The displaced families were moving. Some headed for California where they believed prosperity grew on trees. Others went to Chicago and Detroit, hoping they could find work in factories. It seemed like all of America was in flight. Each night, Ray and Brooks listened to the plight of their unfortunate countrymen on a tiny crystal radio they had built using instructions and drawings that Brooks had copied out of a book in the school library. Brooks heard the stories of the ruin of so many of his countrymen, but he was consumed by his football dreams. However for Ray, the plight of the displaced farmers became his tragedy, too. Empathetically, and almost as deeply as America's dejected and dislodged, Ray was hurting. Every night, he tuned in signals from faraway stations in San Antonio and Fort Worth for news of the migration. He made trips to the school library where he pored over every Depression story in *Life* magazine and *The Saturday Evening Post*. One Saturday a month, Ray and Brooks drove into Junction to the movies. Ray's memories of Tom Mix, and the accompanying collections of outlaws and outrageously overly vilified Indians were overshadowed by the images of the poor Okies he saw in the newsreels. With each passing month, Ray became more consumed by the sad predicament of these people he saw on the giant screen, and with the history of his time.

On some of the fall days after school, Ray would choose a secluded place by the Southern Pacific tracks to see if he could spot unfortunates riding in open boxcars or on the rods underneath the freight trains. Occasionally he would see a transient or two on a train. But if whole families of dispossessed farmers passed through Junction stowed away on the trains of the Southern Pacific, Ray missed seeing them. There was another element of Ray's emotional makeup that helped him feel more miserable that fall. He was restless. Across America, people were moving; history was being made, and Ray felt he was left out of it. With no football, Ray was bored and uneasy, but intensely curious. That curiosity led him down an unexpected path. Ray had never felt particularly close to his father. For most of his youngest son's life, Walter Oakley had sat as the elected head of a court that decided misdemeanors, small civil claims, and had the power to issue restraining orders in domestic abuse matters. Walter was the Justice of the Peace for the southern part of the county. Ray had always known that his father was one of the most important men in their county, and was widely admired, trusted, and counted on by everyone. For Ray, his father's status was just an established fact, something that had always been.

As Ray heard more and more stories about the local victims of the Depression in Kimble County, he was shocked to learn that the man most of them turned to for help was his own father, the man everyone respectfully called Judge Oakley. Ray's concern and curiosity led him to do something that surprised and shocked his father. On the first Saturday in December as Walter went to his car to drive to the small office he kept in Telegraph, and then on to the courtroom and office he occupied at the courthouse in Junction, he found his youngest son sitting in the passenger seat of his car. "You need a ride into Junction this morning, Ray?" Walter asked, momentarily forgetting that his son had asked his parents to call him Amos the way everyone at school was addressing him.

"I thought maybe I could just ride along with you today and see what you do at work," Ray said. He might have added "if that's all right with you," but he didn't.

"Well, I think that's wonderful," Walter beamed, hoping that he was successfully concealing his shock and amazement from the young man.

That Saturday morning, Ray learned that the stories he had heard about his father were absolutely true. All day, he watched as men dressed in worn out overalls and shoes held together with tape or leather strips came to his father desperate, and greatly embarrassed, to ask the judge for advice and help. How could these previously proud men provide food for their hungry children? They and their wives could do without, the men would tell the judge. But they just couldn't bear to watch their kids starve. Several men had been waiting outside Walter's small office in Telegraph, and there was a larger group gathered and waiting when Judge Oakley and his son walked into the big courthouse in Junction. Everyone who came received help. Sometimes Walter would call the pastor of a local church. In other cases, he would call a grocery store and arrange for credit that Walter promised to cover if the man could not eventually pay. And when there was no other option, Walter would reach into his pocket for two, three or even five dollars. "It's a loan," Walter would tell the men.

"But I don't know when I can pay you back," the men would reply.

"Whenever you can, will be soon enough," Walter would assure the despairing neighbor.

If mortgages weren't big problems for Walter's constituents, taxes were. Property taxes had to be paid in cash. And the only thing scarcer than cash in the Texas Hill Country was rain. For at least a dozen neighbors who couldn't pay their tax bills that December, Walter had gone to the bank in Junction to co-sign personal notes that kept their farms from being posted for sale by the sheriff. He wouldn't allow his friends to use their farms as security. Walter guaranteed to pay, if the supplicant could not. Some of the farmers insisted that Walter take produce or chickens. Knowing that the borrower just could not accept charity, even from a close friend, Walter would accept the food, then discretely donate it to churches around Telegraph and Junction. The foodstuffs would then be parceled out by the churches to families whose crops had failed because of the drought.

Early in the morning on the Saturday before Christmas, Ray rode with his father to Junction. They parked in front of the depot a few minutes before the eastbound for San Antonio arrived. Ray had known absolutely nothing about his father's career with the railroad, and he was astounded that everyone at the railroad station seemed to know his father so well. He was shocked when they boarded the train without a ticket. Walter casually displayed a lifetime pass from the Southern Pacific to the conductor on the train, a man too young to have known Walter from his railroading days. But the porter in the club car, where Walter took Ray for a Coca-Cola during the ride, warmly remembered the old friend he called, not judge, but Mr. Walter. The two aging men had ridden together for more than twenty years. "Your daddy and Mr. Easterly built this railroad, long before you were born," the porter explained to the stupefied Ray, who was riding a train for the first time in his life, or at least the first time Ray could remember. As the train edged into San Antonio passing miles of houses and businesses, Ray saw a whole world he had not imagined existed. This new realm he was experiencing would soon magnify Ray's restiveness.

When the train arrived at the station, Walter borrowed a truck from the Southern Pacific, then drove to half a dozen stores collecting boxes of shoes. In some of the stores, Walter paid for what he received, but several of the stores gave Walter five or six pairs. In just over an hour, Walter and Ray had gathered almost twenty pairs of shoes, which they took back to the depot. A man in the express room, someone else Walter seemed to know well, handed father and son two big canvas bags to put the shoes in. "I'll send these back to you on the overnight, Joel," Walter told the man. "No rush," Joel replied. Before Walter could reach down to pick up the two sacks, a giant Black man wearing a red cap took control of the pouches, placed them on a dolly and rolled them away.

"Hold on, Edgar," Walter called to the man, who appeared to be about Ray's father's age. "I'll tag 'em for you, Mr. Walter," the grinning attendant announced, looking back over his shoulder. "That's not what I mean. It's almost Christmas, isn't it?" Walter posed. "Yes sir," Edgar confirmed with an immense smile that highlighted two gold teeth. As Edgar crossed back over to Walter and Ray, Walter placed two silver dollars in his old friend's hand. "Still have children living at home, don't you?" Walter queried. "Mostly grandchildren now," Edgar offered, adding a chuckle to supplement his smile. "Thank you, Mr. Walter and you have a Merry Christmas," the porter concluded. "You too, Edgar," Walter called, as his old friend wheeled the two bags through the double doors. As before, Walter flashed his pass to the conductor, and the two boarded the homebound train without paying.

CHAPTER FOUR

Shortly after the train pulled out of the station, Walter led Ray to the dining car, where they were greeted by yet another attendant, who was also an old friend of Walter's. Ray and Walter both ate hot roast beef sandwiches and mashed potatoes covered with gravy. Occasionally, as the porter came to the table, Walter would joke and reminisce with him about something that had happened ten or fifteen years before Ray had been born. When Walter and Ray arrived back in Junction, there were more than a dozen men waiting for Walter at the courthouse. He carefully went through the bag, selecting the right shoes for each man's children, and handed them over. Some of the men had a homemade cake or a few cookies for Walter, but most had nothing to offer but thanks.

Ray fell into a deep melancholy during Christmas that year. The awareness that there were never again to be any presents from Glenn called up old but wonderful memories of childhood that had been stored far back into the young man's past. Ray also felt weighed down by the suffering and misery pervading the lives of Ray's neighbors. That same dark mood seemed to have infected the entire country. As classes resumed in January, Ray found it progressively harder to concentrate on school. Each train whistle Ray heard brought images into his mind of the millions of hurting and suffering Americans, a great many of whom had become refugees inside their own country. The young high school freshman increasingly felt lured toward a personal, close-up experience of these events, something seemed to be calling to Ray, telling him that he needed to be part of this historic, communal experience. Mrs. Apfel, the librarian, had been shocked by Ray's visits at first, but now had become used to them. In addition to the magazines, Ray was looking at atlases to see where the displaced people had come from, and where they were going. He was also memorizing the routes of the railroads. It seemed to Ray that the Santa Fe, which ran an east-west route several hundred miles north of the Southern Pacific, was likely carrying most of the travelers.

In early February before Ray had boarded the freight train in Junction, he had told no one of his plans—not even Brooks. He left a note in Brooks' locker at school. The note was attached to a letter to his mother explaining that he had to catch up with the history that was going on around them. He also told her not to worry. He could take care of himself. After school and his afternoon workout, Brooks found the letter and took it to his father at his office in the courthouse.

"Don't tell your mother. She won't be able to stand it after what happened to Glenn. She'll die," Brooks' father told him.

"As a matter of fact, I think it would be a good idea if you were to wait here in the office by the phone in case I need you to do something," Walter added. "You tell one of the neighbor boys from school to stop by our house and tell your mother that you and I have important business, that something's come up, and we'll be late getting home," Walter concluded before he walked over to the railroad depot.

"Henson, my son has run off on a freight train," Walter informed the stationmaster.

"Brooks?" the man gasped.

"No, Ray," Walter responded. "I want you to wire west as far as El Paso, and have every freight stopped and searched. Give them Ray's description. When they find him, have them pull him off the train and hold him for me. "I'm going to head west. I'll message you for any news when I get to Del Rio," Walter pleaded.

"When did he leave, Judge?" the stationmaster inquired.

"This morning, we think," Walter replied.

"He hasn't had time to get very far then," Henson suggested. "Don't worry, Judge. I'll take care of it," Henson called as Walter went out the door. Every train was stopped, and every car was searched. It played havoc with the schedules. Hundreds of riders were removed from the trains, but of course Ray was not on any of the trains that had been searched. It was almost nine in the evening before Walter reached Del Rio. He learned the bad news over the telegraph. He asked the stationmaster in Del Rio to let him use the phone to call Brooks.

"Son, we can't find Ray. I'm sure he's all right. I guess he has just given us the slip for the time being," Walter said. Brooks was too frightened to say anything. He was certain his brother was dead.

"I'm going to call Sheriff Wilson and ask him to have one of his men take you home. Tell your mother exactly what has happened without scaring her any more than you have to. Then show her the letter. Tell her that I'm going to ask Sheriff Wilson to wire every county in the state tonight and have a pick-up put out for your brother. I think they'll find him by morning. I'm going to ride the overnight mail train to San Antonio so that I can be ready to ride any direction I need to go to pick Ray up. Ask your mother to have Miguel drive both of you into Junction in the morning. Have her wait at my office so I can phone her as soon as I know something. If she's not too upset, you can go on to school. But otherwise, you stay with her there at the office. Do you understand?"

"Yes sir," Brooks responded.

In a few minutes, Sheriff Wilson arrived in person to drive Brooks home. Ada burst into tears as soon as Brooks and Bill Wilson walked into the house. She had already decided that something terrible had happened. It was Wilson who had come to the house to tell them that Glenn had been killed. Now, she was certain that he had come to tell her that Walter and Ray were dead, too. Ada was not going to stand for it. As soon as she saw Bill Wilson pass through her front door, she rose and walked toward him with her fists clenched. She began pounding the sheriff in the chest with the heels of her closed hands.

"I won't have it, Bill!" she cried out. "I won't have it! You can't take any more of my boys away from me! I simply won't have it!"

After Ada had struck half a dozen blows, the sheriff gently restrained her, wrapping his oversize fingers around the distraught mother's wrists. "It's all right, Ada," he said. "Everything is going to be all right." Ada stopped abruptly and turned on Brooks.

"Where are your father and brother?" she demanded.

"It's all right, Momma," Brooks tried.

"I asked you a question, Brooks Oakley, and I expect an answer right this minute," she ordered.

"Dad's in Del Rio," Brooks responded.

"And where's your brother? Is he dead, or is he in jail?" Ada badgered.

"We don't know where he is, Momma," Brooks answered calmly. "Dad's out looking for him."

"Ada, if you'll sit down for a minute, we'll explain everything to you," Sheriff Wilson coaxed. Ada didn't want to sit down. She wanted to rage at this man who came to her when her sons were in jail or dead. She wanted to be able to control this terrible situation so another son would not be dead. Instead she sat on her sofa, as Brooks calmly related the day's events to her. When he had finished, Brooks handed his mother Ray's letter just as Walter had told him to do. Ada read the letter, then began crying softly. As she cried, her tears fell on the paper, causing some of the ink to run and stain her apron. After a few minutes, Sheriff Wilson saw that Ada was not going to stop crying for some time.

"Brooks," the sheriff said softly as he stood. "I have some work to do helping your father. Tell your mother I'll come by the judge's office as soon as I have some news." Brooks started to stand so that he could walk the sheriff to the door. "Thanks for everything, sheriff," he said. But Sheriff Wilson motioned to Brooks, indicating that he should not rise. "Stay with your mother. I'll see myself out."

CHAPTER FIVE

Another half-hour lapsed before Ray heard a train whistling. As it pulled past, he looked at the lettering on the tender, the car behind the big steam locomotive that carried fuel oil for the engine. *Missouri, Kansas & Texas* it read. Finally, about ten cars behind the locomotive, Ray fixed on a boxcar with an open door. He reached for the floor to vault himself into the boxcar. He winced as the edge of the door on the rolling boxcar nearly took his arm off and sent Ray spinning. He crashed hard onto the rocks of the track ballast. Ray landed, thrust by a force much more severe than any hit he had ever taken on a football field.

Several boxcars with open doors swept past before Ray's head cleared. Regaining his feet, and a vestige of equilibrium, he targeted another likely car and began running alongside, before attempting to reach inside. Timing his speed to match that of the moving train, Ray placed his hands surely, vaulted himself off the ground and fell unceremoniously into the moving car, demonstrating no hint of skill, grace, or style when boarding. Ray spent the next twenty minutes picking splinters out of his hands. Jumping onboard a stopped train in Junction had been vastly easier. Before the train reached New Braunfels, Ray was shivering in a cold wind blowing through the open boxcar. The temperature was plunging, and Ray had left home without a jacket.

———

Walter's train arrived in San Antonio before breakfast. He went straight to the Southern Pacific office and found that the railroad's district executive was waiting for him in his office.

"Practically the whole railroad is looking for him," Walter told his wife, when he called around noon. "And I've talked to Sheriff Wilson two or three times this morning. I wish I knew of something else we could do."

Ada's expression was stern. "I'm coming to San Antonio," she informed her husband.

"I wish you wouldn't," Walter attempted. "There's nothing you can do here, and Ray might turn up where you are."

Ada repeated herself. "I'm coming."

Walter moved on. "Well if you're determined, you should bring Brooks with you," Walter suggested. The stationmaster in Junction wrote passes for Ada and Brooks. By two o'clock, they were on the train. When they reached San Antonio, Walter still had no news about Ray. Walter tried to persuade Ada to go to a hotel, but she wouldn't budge. So, the three of them spent all night in the train master's office waiting for word.

———

Ray closed the door on one side of the boxcar completely and left only a small handhold on the opposite door. To get warm, he moved to the north end of the car. Once the feeling of being cold to the bone faded, a gnawing hunger grabbed Ray. The young adventurer had never considered that what he had undertaken might involve hardship. He had climbed on board that train in Junction answering an undeniable urge to move. Now, he began discovering that wanderlust, the freedom to go where he wanted, when he wanted, had a price. So far, he had faced fear of violence and arrest, cold, and hunger. How had he thought it would be? Certainly not like this, Ray told himself. For ten minutes, the train had been whistling much more regularly, and the sounds from the whistle blasts were lasting longer and longer. Ray guessed that his train was probably nearing Austin. He crawled over to the opening in the door and looked out just as the train slowed for the bridge. For a second, Ray caught sight of the state capitol's shadow in the city lights, just before the big steam engine turned right along West First Street, blocking his view.

Ray remembered what the policeman in San Antonio had told him, that Austin should be fairly safe; but he was taking no chances. Three or four streets after the train crossed the bridge Ray gauged its speed to be ten miles an hour or less. He jumped, stumbled awkwardly, but kept his balance, and ran a few steps until he could stand upright. To Ray's surprise the train was moving down the middle of what appeared to be a major street. He straightened his clothes as he walked beside the moving train, which left Ray behind just as he reached Congress Avenue. The train crossed the avenue and moved right past a big depot, where two passenger trains were loading. Ray looked to his left. Now he could see the state capitol clearly sitting at the north end of a broad thoroughfare. There were streetcars on tracks in the center of the avenue, multicolored taxis, cars and delivery trucks moving in all directions. Office buildings, department stores, and huge movie theaters with elaborate signs illuminated with electric lights. Those movie theaters, all with broad marquees, lined both sides of the wide avenue for several blocks.

Ray was so overwhelmed with excitement at seeing this grand new city that he momentarily forgot his hunger, but a tangy odor from close by reminded him. He looked to his right and saw a tiny but garishly illuminated cart selling hot tamales. They cost five cents a dozen. Ray handed the old Tejano man a nickel for the tamales, then reached into his pocket for another nickel to buy a Nehi orange soda. He had never tasted such wonderful food. Sometimes, Ray had eaten Mexican food with Miguel when he was working in the fields, but he had never experienced food more savory than the spicy hot tamales. He wolfed down the first dozen in just a few minutes. "Can I buy less than twelve?" Ray asked the man.

"How many?" the man asked in Spanish. Like almost everyone else in his family, Ray had never learned more than a few Spanish words, but he guessed at what the question had been.

"Three," he said, then repeated the word in Spanish.

"Two cents," the man responded in Spanish. Ray passed over the two pennies, and the empty Nehi bottle.

"Could I have another Nehi?" he asked, handing the man an additional nickel. The vendor had given Ray four tamales. He barely managed to get down the last one, then swallowed the final third of his cold drink in a single gulp. Ray wanted to walk up the avenue to the capitol building but changed his mind when he noticed a policeman walking six or eight blocks up the street. Ray decided that he probably could not get past the cop without being questioned. So instead of walking up Congress Avenue, he followed the tracks along the street where the freight train had disappeared earlier.

Ray walked less than ten minutes before he caught up with the parked train. A lone security detective raked a nightstick across the cars as he passed. No one jumped from the train. Ray measured the man's demeanor and concluded that it was unlikely that the guard would chase anyone who ran. As the railroad agent passed to the other side of the train, Ray followed his steps and the sound of the stick against the freight cars. Ray stopped to relieve himself beside an open boxcar before climbing in. His hands were almost raw from all the splinters he had picked up the last time he had boarded the train. The inside of the boxcar was totally dark. Ray couldn't hear anything, but he walked around the perimeter of the car's interior to make sure no one else was inside the car. Becoming more cautious, he noted some boards from old packing crates in the car.

Ray was not cold so long as the train stood still. Remembering how he had nearly frozen three hours earlier, Ray set about closing the car before the train pulled out. He propped a board from the packing crates in each of the doors, so no one could lock him inside. Ray heard a long blast from the whistle. Then, the cars jerked as the brakes released. The movement rippled along the whole length of the train. The engineer blew for each crossing, more than a dozen in all, before the train finally began to gather speed. Ray moved to the north end of the car and tried to make himself comfortable. A hundred fifty miles to the southwest, Ray's warm bed was neatly made and empty. When he closed his eyes, Ray could almost see Brooks asleep in his bed across their room. Ray could never have imagined that his brother was wide awake on a hard bench in a railroad office in San Antonio. Nor could Ray have envisioned that Brooks, completely convinced that Ray was dead, was consumed with agony for himself, and for his parents.

CHAPTER SIX

The Katy rolled on through the chilly Central Texas night. Even though the freight was a local, there was nothing to put off and nothing to take on in either Round Rock or Georgetown. Ray fell into a deep sleep as the train stopped in Belton to change crews and wait for a passenger train. As he slept, he dreamed he was back in the police car in San Antonio. Just as he heard the officer's warning about Temple again, Ray felt the whack of an ax handle against his thigh. A second blow struck his rib cage on the other side. Ray raised up struggling to determine what had gone wrong with his dream and was jolted by a gruff voice.

"On your feet, boy. You're way too big for us to pick up and throw off the train," the voice growled.

Ray jerked an ax handle. As he shot to his feet, he upended the big railroad bull holding the bottom of the cudgel and sent him sprawling onto the floor of the boxcar. Ray stumbled forward toward the open door and was hammered by a blow from a second ax handle that landed directly between his shoulder blades and crashed him onto the rocky roadbed below. Blood gushed from Ray's nose, knees, and elbows, and his clothes were ripped by the razor-edged rocks.

"No," Ray heard a panicked voice scream, followed in a fraction of a second by the crack of a gunshot. "Not here, you idiot. You can't shoot him here in the yard," warned a different, unidentified voice in a roared command. Ray looked over his shoulder and saw one of the guards poised to shoot his pistol a second time and watched in horror as a cohort shoved the gunman's arm to disrupt his aim. Ray scrambled to his feet and ran as fast as he could. As the second shot went wild, Ray escaped into the darkness. There, for the first time, the young adventurer considered the option of going home.

Ray stood on the edge of the freight yard, remaining disoriented for a long time. Summoning a lot of concentration, Ray was eventually able to reconstruct where the train must have entered the yard. He found the main line and began walking north, assuming that the junction with the Santa Fe would be north of the yard. There was no particular reason for Ray's assumption. There was nothing to even confirm that Ray was in Temple. However, his guesses turned out to be accurate. The Katy yard was quite small compared to the Santa Fe yard, which began about a half-mile northwest of the junction of the two lines.

As Ray entered the yard, a freight was moving southeast toward the Texas coast. Three trains with locomotives appeared ready to head northwest, while a switch engine worked, building a train. Ray saw an open boxcar on one of the trains. Feeling the pain in his leg, he positioned his hands to vault into the car, but hesitated. Remembering the advice of the policeman in San Antonio, Ray changed his mind and walked quietly along the main line for nearly three miles before he found a bend on an upgrade. As the first traces of sun rays appeared, Ray took a spot beneath a trestle where he could wait for one of the trains to chug out of the yard. In less than ten minutes, he heard the first faint whistles from the locomotive blowing at crossings. As soon as he heard the engine cross the trestle, Ray emerged from his hiding place and began looking for a car with an open door. About thirty cars behind the tender, he spotted a boxcar with a door open. The train was moving twelve to fifteen miles per hour, despite the grade. Ray timed the arrival of the car, began running at full speed and moved toward the train as soon as he saw the approaching door. He placed his hands on the floor of the boxcar and pushed himself up as hard as he could.

His entry was a little more graceful than his last two leaps had been, but he still filled his palms with splinters. He also tore open the gash on his right knee.

It took almost twenty minutes for Ray to pick out the splinters and stop the bleeding. He was thirsty but had nothing to drink. He closed the doors on the car and found a corner to sleep in. By the time he woke, the train had moved far into west Texas, meaning that Ray had slept through the vast Santa Fe complex in Fort Worth without further consequences. Ray's knees and hands were extremely sore. He was hungry; and by now, his thirst had become critical. The sun was almost directly overhead, and it was unbearably hot inside the car. Ray slid open one of the doors, and began studying the red soil and mesquite, hoping that he could somehow divine where he was. The train rolled on and on.

With the afternoon almost gone, Ray knew he had to get off the train. For several hours, he had been trying without success to catch a glimpse of the front of the train, hoping to spot a town where he could exit. When the blasts from the engine's whistle quickened, Ray decided that the train was approaching a place with more than one crossing. The train, which had never exceeded thirty miles per hour, ultimately slowed to fifteen miles per hour. Trying to protect his knee from further injury, Ray looked carefully for a spot and jumped. He hit soft earth and rolled. Ray avoided hurting his knee again; but when he stood, he was covered with red dust. The young man brushed and beat his pants as much as he could, but there was no way to get all the dirt out. Ray tucked his shirt in and tried to straighten his hair. Despite his considerable efforts, he was a total mess. Ray looked very much like a bum, who had just ridden into Lubbock on a freight train.

CHAPTER SEVEN

As he walked past the window of the cafe, Ray saw his reflection. If they would not serve him in the restaurant, Ray hoped they would at least give him a glass of water. For the last two years, the owner of the cafe had been visited by a lot of adolescent transients, some even younger than Ray. Instead of scolding his youthful customer, the man directed Ray to the bathroom where he could wash his face and hands. When Ray came out, there was a hamburger steak smothered with mushroom gravy, mashed potatoes, a plate of dinner rolls, and a glass of buttermilk waiting for him at the counter. There was no one else in the restaurant. It took Ray less than ten minutes to eat everything in front of him. "How much do I owe you?" Ray asked the owner.

"Ain't no dishes for you to wash, 'cause there ain't been no customers," the man replied. Ray put a dollar bill on the counter. The owner was shocked to see the money. He had served a lot of youngsters passing through, but Ray was the first who had ever actually produced money to pay.

"Is that enough?" Ray asked.

"Sure son. Plate lunch is only thirty-five cents," the man said.

"Then could I have another one?" Ray asked quietly, a request that sent the owner into the kitchen to dish up another hamburger steak and more mashed potatoes.

"Do you want more buttermilk?" the man asked, and Ray nodded.

"And some water would be nice, too," he said. After Ray had finished the second lunch, the second glass of buttermilk and four glasses of water, the man put a big slice of apple pie on the counter.

"No charge," he said. "You want coffee?" the man asked, as Ray attacked the pie.

Ray nodded again, and the owner went to get two cups of coffee out of the big stainless-steel urn: one for Ray and one for himself.

"Where you headed? California?" he asked.

"Yes sir," Ray replied.

"There's no work out there. It's not like you've heard," the cafe owner told him. Ray didn't answer. "If you've got another fifty cents, I know where you can get some better clothes," the man said.

"I'm afraid they'd just get torn up, too," Ray responded. "Well, you can get a denim jacket for a quarter," the man suggested. Ray recalled how cold he'd been in those freight cars at night, but then he considered how much sunshine there was supposed to be in California.

"I don't think I'll need one," Ray asserted.

"Suit yourself," the man concluded. Instead of refreshing Ray, the meal made him realize how much he missed the regular comforts he had at home. Was there really any point to this trip? His mind was filled with doubt as he walked back toward the rail yard. All he had to do was pick up the phone and place a call to his father's office in Junction, and he could return to his bed, regular meals, and get away from the threats of beating or death. The reality of Ray's adventure was a long way from what he had imagined in his many daydreams. Perhaps he hadn't really given this journey a fair chance, Ray thought, as he debated his situation in a silent discussion taking place inside his head. What he wanted to see was in California, and Ray was not even out of Texas. In fact, he was still a long way from being out of Texas.

There had never been a time like this before, and it seemed unlikely that there would ever be another. This was Ray's one chance to see this moment in history. With that thought in his head, Ray spotted a Santa Fe freight starting north and vaulted into an open boxcar. He felt intense pain from his ripped knees as they bumped onto the floor of the car. Ray had been so absorbed with his thoughts that he had forgotten the warning he had received in San Antonio. Without thinking, Ray had boarded a car rolling through the freight yards in Lubbock. Immediately, he looked around the car to make sure there were no security people inside. Then, he peered out quickly, trying to keep as much of his head inside the car as possible. He scanned both sides of the train in that manner, looking for detectives. Ray saw none, but kept checking every few minutes until he felt the train pick up speed as it rolled into the open countryside of the Panhandle.

Everywhere Ray looked was mostly bare flat red earth, and dust blew with only an occasional, brief pause. Every few miles, the train passed a cluster of empty farm buildings. Ray suspected that these farms had belonged to people who had been "dusted out." That's what the magazine articles called it when a family lost its farm because of the weather and the Depression. All the magazines Ray had read were filled with the tragic stories of farmers who had been forced off their land at the point of a gun by the sheriff. The same magazines carried stark black and white photographs of dust storms and empty farmhouses and buildings. The vacant farms passing in front of Ray as he rode through the Panhandle weren't gray, but a bizarre red. The houses and the buildings were coated with red dust. Sometimes, the dust built up against barbed wire fences, utility poles, and abandoned tractors or cars.

Not every farm was abandoned. Perhaps one in three showed signs of life—animals in the barnyard, wash on the line turning red from the blowing dust, small vegetable plots. Sometimes Ray even saw evidence of cotton that had been harvested in the fall. He saw one man plowing a field with a mule. Ray witnessed another half-dozen farmers plowing with ancient tractors, but most of the agricultural buildings and houses the train passed were empty. Ray stared out over the Panhandle until the setting sun appeared to fall off the horizon and into New Mexico, leaving behind only a few shadows.

Ray moved back inside the car. As he had learned to do earlier, he closed both doors almost shut, propping them just slightly open with abandoned lumber from packing crates that had been left behind. Once the sun was down, the warmth of the day disappeared quickly. Ray realized too late that he had made a mistake by not spending a quarter for a jacket. He told himself that if he ever did anything like this again, he would bring a coat and some extra clothes. Before the cold began to seriously affect him, Ray felt the train slow and heard a whistle sound for a third time in quick succession, indicating a city. Ray slid the door open wide enough to get his head out. He could see light escaping through the windows of houses, and from electric lamps mounted on metal arms extending from creosote poles. Ray waited a couple of minutes, and opened the opposite door so he could look out the other side of the train. Now, the whistling had become almost constant, as the shadowed outlines of buildings in downtown Amarillo came into view. Ray wished the train would slow down before he tried to jump, but he didn't want to be onboard the train when it reached the freight yard. Ray had already had too much contact with the railroad security people. Half-a-mile south of downtown, the tracks turned to the east in a broad arc, and the train slowed, its speed dropping below ten miles per hour. Ray jumped out past the rocks. His legs were moving when his feet hit the ground, and he was able to keep his balance by running at full speed. This was only the second time Ray had gotten off a moving train without either being hurt or covered with dirt. Of course, his clothes were still torn from earlier boardings and exits, and he had enough growth of beard so that his appearance left little doubt that Ray Oakley was a young man traveling by freight train—a bum.

He moved away from the track to a nearby street and began following roughly the route the train was taking toward the freight yards. Ray thought briefly about spending the night somewhere in or near Amarillo but decided that it was a good time to catch a westbound train for California.

CHAPTER EIGHT

Lights in the houses Ray walked past were beginning to flicker out. The nighttime air in the Texas Panhandle was icy cold and made worse by a brutish north wind. The young man again wished he had bought the recommended coat in Lubbock. Ray's passage in the night occasionally brought a dog outside to investigate. Other dogs barked a few times until Ray had passed out of their territory. Otherwise, he was alone on the street.

Ray had walked within sight of the giant freight yard when he was caught in the headlights of a car. The lights dimmed, and the car drove past him. In a few seconds, Ray heard the car stop and turn around. He was lit by the headlights a second time. The car moved slowly past Ray and halted. The black Ford sedan had four doors, and it was only two or three years old. Ray saw the door of the car open, and a man wearing khaki pants, a jacket, and a felt cowboy hat, stepped out. Ray guessed the man was just a bit younger than his father. He was trim, fit, smiling, and spoke in a friendly tone.

"Hi, son. You all right?" he inquired, his demeanor and voice low-key.

"Yes sir," Ray answered cautiously.

"You been traveling?" the man continued. Ray surmised that this man was well practiced in situations like this. He knew how to make strangers feel at ease.

"Yes sir," Ray repeated.

"Could you come up to the front of the car, here, so I can see you in the light, please?" the man requested with a smile. Ray was suspicious. The stranger seemed all right, but he was too curious. Ray hesitated. "I'm Chief Jim Garrett of the Potter County Sheriff's Office," the man explained with no hint of threat or intimidation. Ray, hoping to keep this from turning into a confrontation, walked reluctantly into the car's headlights. "Going to California?" the chief asked.

"Yes sir," Ray replied.

"Looks like you've had a pretty rough trip so far," the chief suggested. "If you're going to keep doing this, you might want to get a little better at it," the chief observed. "You cold?" he asked Ray, after a pause. Ray nodded, dismayed that this mysterious man could read him so easily. "I didn't catch your name," the chief remarked, casually.

"Ray," the shivering young adventurer responded.

"Wouldn't be Ray Oakley, would it?" the chief asked.

"Yes sir," Ray confirmed, astonished.

"Well I guess everybody in Texas is looking for you," the chief announced. "I was on my way home for a late supper. You wanna come along?" the chief invited. Ray hesitated. "Course I could hold you at the jail, but I don't suppose that will be necessary," the lawman observed almost offhandedly. The chief popped open the front passenger door. In no more than five seconds, the law enforcement officer had closed Ray's door, walked around the front of the car, and slipped behind the wheel, never losing sight of the young Mr. Oakley. Ray had been poised to run, but something had told him that wouldn't work.

"I'm kinda hungry," the chief said easily, displaying another friendly smile as Ray sat anxiously in the passenger seat. "We usually have tamales on Tuesdays," the chief informed his newly invited dinner guest. You like tamales?" he posed.

"Yes sir," Ray responded, recalling how good the tamales he had eaten in Austin had been. The lawman backed the Ford into an arc, then pulled it forward, so the car was headed the same direction as it had been when he had initially spotted Ray. After they had driven through the darkness for about two minutes, Ray finally spoke.

"Do you catch criminals this easy?" he inquired.

"Sometimes," Garrett laughed. A few minutes later, the chief swung the Ford into the driveway of a small frame house. Ray suspected that he had walked past it shortly after jumping from the train. "Mother," the chief called out as the two walked into the house. "This is Ray Oakley. I hope he'll be staying with us a day or two. He was on his way to California, but I think his daddy wants him back down in Junction."

"How do you do?" Sylvia Garrett asked.

"Fine, ma'am," Ray answered.

"You're a nice-looking young man, but you're kind of a mess," Mrs. Garrett suggested, a warm smile lighting her face, offering comfort and expressing cordiality.

"Yes, ma'am," Ray agreed.

"I'll bring him some fresh clothes from the jail, when I come home," Jim told his wife. "I've been telling Ray about your tamales," Jim Garrett continued. "From the looks of him, he could eat about three dozen by himself." Everyone laughed.

"They're hot," Sylvia proclaimed. "I'll get them on the table while y'all get washed up." The chief showed Ray to the bathroom, where the youngster cleaned the railroad dirt and soot from his face, arms and hands. When Ray came back into the living room, the chief was on the telephone.

"Yes sir, it's him all right," the deputy was saying. "Yes sir, I believe you can call the judge and tell him he can come on up," the chief answered, then paused while the person on the other end apparently asked another question. "Oh, he's got a few cuts, and his britches are torn, but he's safe and sound," Chief Garrett explained. "Well, I thought he could stay here with me," he suggested in answer to another question. "No. There's no need to keep him in jail" the chief responded, as he looked directly at Ray. "I don't think you'll run. Will you, son?" he asked. Ray shook his head. "No sir. He won't run. There's no need to lock him up," Chief Garrett confirmed.

Ray, almost begging with his eyes, motioned for the chief to cover the mouthpiece of the phone. Embarrassed, Ray's voice cracked as he began to speak. "My father doesn't have to come all the way up here," he pleaded. "I've got money. I promise I'll buy a ticket and go back home on the next train."

"Just a minute, sheriff," the chief requested. "I trust you, Ray. And I suppose if I had arrested you for a crime, I'd let you do it. But your daddy's worried sick about you. He's sent us two or three wires already. From what we hear, the judge is a good man, and he asked us to hold you until he can come get you. "I guess you're embarrassed. But if the judge asked us to hold on to you, then I expect we should."

"Hold on again, Sheriff," the chief said into the phone a second time.

"Why would you let me go on my own, if I were a criminal?" Ray asked.

"Because if you were an offender, and you didn't keep your word, I could track you down and stomp you. But you haven't done anything but run away, and I wouldn't stomp a boy for running away," the lawman explained. Ray clearly would do anything to have his plea accepted. He was humiliated at the thought of his father coming to Amarillo to get him, but he saw it was no use.

"I'm sorry, Sheriff," the chief continued. "I was having a conversation with Ray. Well, he wanted to go home on his own. But I explained to him that he needed to wait here for the judge to pick him up. No sir, I'm sure he'll be all right here. We don't have to lock him up. He's an honest boy. You can tell that by looking at him. He won't run," the chief finished, then hung up the phone. "Let's see about those tamales," Jim Garrett suggested, turning to Ray.

CHAPTER NINE

Ray only picked at the tamales. He had been hungry before he came out of the bathroom. But the idea that his father would soon be on a train for Amarillo consumed Ray, and he couldn't concentrate on the food. The Garretts attempted to engage their young guest in a pleasant conversation during the meal, but Ray seemed to be lost in his own thoughts. The chief and his wife understood. After the second time they asked Ray a question and he did not respond, the couple confined their talking to one another. Chief and Mrs. Garrett discussed rooming and meal arrangements for Ray, but he did not seem to hear. The phone rang just as the chief was finishing his meal, but Ray apparently did not hear that either.

"It's for you, Ray," the chief informed him. "Ray, the phone is for you," the chief called out after Ray had not responded to his first summons. Ray looked up and walked slowly toward the chief, who was holding the phone for him. Ray took the instrument into his hands, his thoughts apparently still a million miles away.

"Hello," he answered distantly.

"Ray, is that you?" Ada asked.

"Yes ma'am," he responded weakly.

"Oh Ray," she proclaimed, expressing both relief and exasperation.

"I can't believe you would do something like this to me." A tear ran down Ray's cheek, and he could not speak. Before launching his grandiose and selfish scheme, Ray had not once considered what should have been the obvious fact that his mother would be devastated by his disappearance. The sound of Ada's voice immediately inundated Ray with regret. "Are you all right?" his mother inquired. Ray tried to speak but still was unable. "Are you okay?" Ada asked again with obvious concern.

"Yes ma'am," Ray finally managed, fighting to hold back sobs. There was a long silence on the phone.

"Here's your father," Ada surrendered and passed the equipment to her husband.

"The sheriff says you're all right. Is that the case?" Walter asked.

Ray was swallowing his tears as quickly as he could. He continued to struggle with an inability to speak, and it took him almost a minute to get words out. "Yes sir," he finally responded.

"I'll be up to get you, tomorrow or Thursday, depending on how the train schedules work," Walter informed his son.

Tears were flooding down Ray's cheeks. Walter, waiting for a reply, could only hear the faint sounds of his son crying at the other end of the phone.

"Are you all right?" Walter asked in a tone of voice indicating his increasing concern.

"Papa?" Ray asked.

"Yes?"

"Can I come home on my own?"

Now the pause was on Walter's end of the call. He appreciated how humiliated his son must be. It might be better to let him come home by himself. Then, Walter looked across the room at his wife. Ada was at the edge of her capacity to endure. Only Glenn's death had been worse for his wife than Ray's disappearance. "I'm not sure your mother could stand the apprehension and uncertainty, if I said yes to your request," Walter suggested after a long pause of his own.

"But I will come home. I promise," Ray said.

Walter sensed how desperate Ray sounded, and he was torn between two loyalties. Was he going to do something that was extremely important to his son—something that might help build trust between Walter and Ray, something that might even help this restless boy grow up and learn to be more considerate of others? On the other hand, how much was Walter prepared to add to his wife's pile of burdens? "Let me talk to your mother, and I'll call you back," Ray's father told him. "Could I speak to the deputy again, please?" Walter asked Ray.

"Yes sir," Ray replied and handed the phone back to the chief.

In about ten minutes the phone rang again. "It's for you, Ray," the chief deputy offered. His mother was on the other end of the phone a second time.

"Amos Ray Oakley," she spoke sternly. "Your father has been trying to convince me that we should allow you to buy a ticket and come home on your own. He says that will be best for you. He says that you will be embarrassed to death, if he rides the train up to Amarillo to get you. What I think is that I should come up there and get you myself," Ada announced. Ray could not speak. "You have until Thursday night to get back here," Ada told her son tersely, before she hung up the phone. A few minutes later, the phone rang again, and Ray's heart sank. He was afraid his mother had changed her mind.

But this phone call was from Walter. He told the chief they had decided to let Ray come home on his own. "But would you do me two favors?" Walter requested.

"Yes sir," the chief agreed.

"Would you see to it that my son buys a ticket, and does not try to get home on freight trains?" Walter asked.

"Yes sir," the chief promised. "And could I impose upon you to put him on the train, yourself?" Walter continued.

"Yes sir," the lawman affirmed.

"Thank you very much, Chief Garrett," Walter said. "I really appreciate what you have done for us, and I'm sorry we have put you to so much trouble," Walter apologized.

"No trouble at all, judge. Don't worry about Ray. He'll be just fine," the chief said.

Early Wednesday morning, Brooks drove his father to his office in Junction then returned to the farm for his mother, who had stayed behind to get Ruth off to school. Walter was on the phone when they arrived at Walter's courthouse office. As usual, there were four or five people sitting in chairs lined against the wall by the door waiting to see the judge. Brooks and Ada walked directly over to Walter's desk. "Thanks chief," Walter said into the phone. "I'm sorry we kept you up so late. Goodbye."

"Ray got on a train to Fort Worth at 1:30 this morning," Walter told Ada and Brooks.

"Thank goodness," Ada sighed. Walter believed that she still felt it had been a bad idea to allow Ray to come home on his own.

"Papa, I can stay and help, if you need me," Brooks offered.

"No son, you go on to school," Walter told Brooks.

"Do you need anything, Momma?" Brooks asked considerately.

"No. You run on to school," Ada replied mechanically.

Walter and Ada needed to talk. Rather than inconvenience the people in his office by asking them to wait outside, Walter led Ada down the hall to the empty courtroom used by the district judge for trials and by the county commissioners for their meetings. Ada never interfered with Walter's work, but she hated it—hated it because it was politics. She didn't mind that Walter spent most of his time helping the people of the county with their problems. The farm made a good living, and they could afford it. She didn't mind that he was always loaning someone money that frequently could not be repaid. They had a lot more than most people, and Ada agreed that they could share what they had. What Ada despised was the politics. She hated that she couldn't sit in her husband's office and talk without the whole county listening in. She hated the men who came to her house, often at night, from all over Texas, smoking cigars, slapping Walter on the back, and promising to do all kinds of things they would never do. She hated their loud talk and crude language.

Walter was an honest and decent man. Ada felt the politicians took advantage of her husband, and that made her angry. Ada also hated the way Walter patronized her when she tried to talk to him about these concerns. When the door to the courtroom closed behind them, Ada's frustration spilled out. "Marion Walter," she began, choking back tears. "Here we are facing one of the biggest crises of our life, and we can't even sit down and talk about it because of your damned politics." Walter was shocked. He had heard Ada scold the children using their middle names, when she was particularly angry, but she had only called him by his full name at their wedding. Walter was astonished. He had never heard Ada say "damned" before. He reached to put his hand on her shoulder to comfort her, but she knocked it away.

For fifteen minutes, Ada recounted her frustrations about politics and the disappointments they had suffered with Ralph, Glenn, Maryon, Jimmie, and now with Ray. At the end, sitting at the table used by the defendant and his attorney during trials, Ada's head fell into her hands. "I just can't take it this time," she sobbed. "Not Ray. I have spent half my life sitting up at night nursing him back from near death, and now he has run away. I can't take it," she gasped, as the crying destroyed her capacity to speak.

Walter, sitting in the wooden chair beside her, was shaken. It had never occurred to him that there was anything on earth this strong woman next to him couldn't take. He had gotten through the crisis by using his routine, the tools of his office. He had been busy sending wires and making calls to his friends all over Texas to get Ray home safely. He had been scared, but his activity had saved him from giving in to his fears. Now that Ada had seemingly crumbled, Walter wasn't sure he could maintain his composure, either. Ada was the strongest person he had ever known—stronger than his father, stronger even than the great Mescalero chief Walter had faced as a boy. If she couldn't take this, Walter feared that he, too, might collapse. Walter took a deep breath, stood up, and walked out to the water fountain in the hall. He swished the water around in his mouth several times, then headed back into the courtroom. When he returned, Ada was sitting straight up. Her eyes were dry.

"I'm sorry," she said.

"That's quite all right," Walter said evenly. He wanted to reach over, hug his wife, and assure her that everything was going to work out. However, as soon as he sat down, she stood up.

"I'm going to McLane's. The girls and I will need new dresses for Easter, and I'd better get started on them," Ada declared, then paused at the door. "I'll be back around eleven. I believe you should get word to the school for Brooks to come drive me home during lunch," Ada directed. Walter was amazed. Easter was the one time of the year they splurged. For years, he had been taking Ada into San Antonio on the train a month before Easter, so she could buy new dresses for the girls and herself at Joske's. Now, she was marching across the square to buy material to make four dresses. He sat for a minute wondering at Ada. He decided that whatever had led her to alter her routine was something he should stay far away from.

Walter finally rose from his chair and walked to his office. The phone had been ringing the whole time Walter had been gone. One of the farm women, who had been waiting to see the judge, sat nervously behind his desk answering a call. In front of her was a list of neatly written names. Some of the names belonged to people from out of town. She had written the phone numbers next to the names. The woman noticed Walter, when he was about two-thirds of the way across his office. She jumped out of her chair so suddenly that she nearly knocked the phone down. In a continuous movement, she thrust the phone into Walter's hands, and raced back to the chair against the wall, where she had been sitting when Ada and Brooks arrived. The woman was nearly fifty years old, and she looked more like seventy. The expression on her face gave the impression of a seven-year-old child who had been caught doing something that she knew would get her in trouble. That chair belonged to a great and important man, and the woman felt that she had been presumptuous. Walter gave his constituent a warm, grateful smile, hoping to communicate that she had done nothing wrong. He would thank her for taking his messages just as soon as he finished his phone call.

CHAPTER TEN

Just before five o'clock, Ray's train moved past the giant grain elevators and steamed toward downtown Fort Worth. The restless adventurer was still sound asleep several minutes after the train pulled into the station. The stocky man in a wrinkled blue suit had nudged him several times before the exhausted young traveler opened his eyes.

"Are you Ray Oakley?" Ray heard him ask. "I'm Chief Deputy Sam Vines of the Tarrant County Sheriff's Office," the chief said. Ray was groggy, and his eyes were still not fully open. He slowly rose to his feet while frantically rummaging through his pockets, searching for the letter Chief Garrett had given him in Amarillo. At last Ray found the document, and in a befuddled state, thrust it at the man. The chief opened the letter, gave it a quick glance, and smiled at Ray, whose eyes were beginning to focus on the lawman's ruddy face and his salt and pepper hair.

"I'm not here to arrest you. Sheriff just thought it might be a good idea if I stopped by to make sure you caught the train for San Antone," the chief explained.

"Did my father ask that you do this?" Ray croaked in a voice just above a whisper. His speech pattern was disoriented. He was still in a sleep related fog.

"No, sheriff just felt we should offer the courtesy. We think a lot of the judge up here. Fort Worth is a big city, and we wouldn't want anything to happen to you while you're here. I'm not going to harm you," the very friendly sounding man added after a brief pause. Moments later, Ray was walking through a waiting room with the chief. The place was cavernous, overwhelming in size and lavishness. Ray followed the deputy to the ticket counter. Several people were in line ahead of him. When his turn came, the agent took Ray's ticket and began looking at it sternly.

"Who wrote this, son?" the agent asked Ray after studying the document for perhaps a minute and a half.

"Someone in Amarillo," Ray replied.

"Well, he didn't know a hoot n' holler about what he was doing," the man proclaimed. "He's got you sitting here for a good four hours, when you could be riding. I'm going to straighten this out for you," the agent told Ray.

The authoritative gentleman on the other side of the counter adjusted his eyeshade, took a new blank ticket form, and began furiously writing numbers and words in the spaces. When he completed the first form, he took another from a box on the desk and filled in more numbers and words. Next, he focused on Ray's old ticket, attached it to the second form and slammed them together with a stapler. He tossed those papers in another box on the desk and shoved the new ticket under the barred window at Ray with its top leaf folded back.

"I've got you on the Number Seven for Dallas. It leaves through there in about twenty minutes," the ticket agent said, pointing to a giant archway. "You've got time for coffee, but no more. At Union Station," the agent paused to look at Ray's face. "You're not from around here, are you?" he asked. Ray shook his head. "At Union Station, that's in Dallas," he resumed, "you catch Katy train Number Six. That'll take you all the way to San Antone. There, you get on the *Limited* and ride it to Junction." The agent pointed at some big doors across the waiting room. "Train's out there," he said. "Remember, you just got time for coffee," the man reminded.

"Thanks," Ray confirmed.

"No bags?" the agent inquired, peering over his glasses.

"No sir," Ray said.

"Next!" the agent called, looking at a woman standing behind the chief.

Deputy Vines led Ray through some more doors. Above the doors, *Coffee Shop* was etched on the glass in the transom. The chief found two seats at the counter. Ice water, napkins, and spoons appeared in front of them at once. "Two coffees," the chief said. "And one apple pie," he added. "I suppose you can slam down some pie at the same time you drink your coffee?" the chief challenged Ray with a knowing smile. Ray was starving and made no protest to the offer of free food. He was still disoriented from sleeping on the train, but he felt a growing suspicion inside that his father was manipulating his whole ride home. Being arrested by the chief deputy in Amarillo, that was an accident. But being greeted by the chief deputy in Fort Worth, surely his father was behind that.

"And my father didn't send you?" Ray asked Chief Vines again.

"No son," he answered kindly. "I told you. We heard you were coming in a call from the sheriff's office in Amarillo."

Ray's face held a puzzled expression. "Maybe he told them to tell you?" Ray suggested.

"Nope," Vines asserted, maintaining his pleasant demeanor. "Chief Garrett is a cautious man. He didn't think you'd run when you got here. But when he called, he said it wouldn't hurt to check on you," the deputy patiently explained. "I suspect that the chief also figured that you might not be experienced in big city train stations and might never have dealt with the complications of catching passenger trains in Fort Worth or Dallas."

How could his father be so important and powerful? Ray had never paid much attention to the people running for office who came to visit his father. He shared his mother's dislike for politicians. At home, Ray considered his father's status in the county a bit of an embarrassment.

Ray had been amazed at the respect the railroad people in San Antonio had shown his father. Now, here he was in another major city, sitting with one of the most important lawmen in Fort Worth. Ray couldn't figure out why these people would go to so much trouble for Walter Oakley. This new puzzle temporarily replaced Ray's worry about how neighbors back home in Telegraph and Junction were going to react to his return. Ray ate the last bite of pie just as the chief finished his coffee. The chief slid a dollar bill across the counter. Some change came back, and Chief Vines left a dime for a tip. In a few minutes, Ray and the chief had walked through the waiting room and onto the platform. He showed his ticket to the porter and stepped up. As Ray turned, Chief Vines extended his hand. "Good luck," the chief said, shaking Ray's hand.

"Thanks for the pie" Ray responded and boarded the train for Dallas. In what had now become a familiar routine, Ray heard the whistle, then the conductor's distinctive call. "All aboard." In a few minutes, steam began to hiss, and slowly the wheels on the huge Texas & Pacific locomotive turned. More whistles. The locomotive picked up speed, and the train headed for Dallas. Ray changed trains in Dallas without any assistance from law enforcement. He kept his eyes alert for more cops in Waco and Austin but was not bothered. As the MK&T's Number Six rolled south out of Austin, Ray began wondering if there would be a deputy to see him from train to train in San Antonio, or if perhaps his father would be there to meet the train. However, just as in Dallas, Ray left the train without anyone approaching. It was a few minutes after nine in the morning, when Ray stepped onto the platform in San Antonio.

The Katy from Dallas to San Antonio had taken the entire night to travel three hundred miles. Just as scheduled, it had stopped in every town between Dallas and Austin, but hardly anyone got on the train and few got off. Mostly, the train was dropping off and picking up mail. By the time Ray arrived in San Antonio, he was starving. There had been no food available along the way. Ray took his remaining ninety cents to a small cafe across from the depot, where he ate four eggs, sausage, biscuits, potatoes, milk, and coffee. An hour later, he was on the *Sunset Limited* heading home.

CHAPTER ELEVEN

The only time Ray had seen his mother cry had been when Glenn died, and he was desperately hoping that she wouldn't cry when Ray got home. The last ten miles of the ride into Junction had seemed like it was taking days. Finally in mid-afternoon, the train stopped, and it took a full minute for Ray to muster the will to stand up and walk shakily onto the wooden passenger platform at the little station his father had built several years before Ray was born. He looked for his parents and Brooks, but no one was there to meet him. Ray's next step was to walk to his father's office in the courthouse. But once there, he found the door was locked, and no one was around. Ray thought about walking to school to wait, and ride home with Brooks. But he didn't want to be seen by any of the other kids.

This was not at all what the Oakleys' youngest son had expected. The walk home would take Ray about three hours, so it would be after dark when he got there. Ray also considered, then rejected, stopping by the sheriff's office to see if his father had left any instructions. After standing in front of the locked door for better than five minutes, Ray left the courthouse and began the long walk to the farm. Ray had walked just over an hour, when an old Ford truck appeared ahead of him. Within a moment, Miguel Velasquez had pulled to a stop beside him. He motioned for Ray to get in, but did not speak. Ray climbed into the truck. Miguel turned the truck around and headed back toward the farm. After he had finished shifting gears, Miguel handed his bewildered passenger an envelope with Ray's name written on it. The young man's hands trembled as he recognized his mother's handwriting. Ray paused for several seconds before carefully opening the envelope, wishing to keep this important letter as neat as possible. After reading only one sentence, he gasped for breath, trying as hard as he could not to cry in front of Miguel. Ray's eyes became clouded with water, but the tears didn't flow down his cheeks.

Dear Ray,

You have broken my heart.

I am glad you are safe. But you must learn not to be reckless with your life, or I fear you will wind up dead, the same way your brother did. I have not spent hundreds of nights sitting up nursing you to keep you alive so that you can throw that precious life away foolishly.

If you love me or appreciate anything your father and I have done for you, you will let this episode be the only one of its kind. You will settle down, start to work hard in school, and see if you can't amount to something. I would like you to live long enough to make me proud of you and not wind up dead in a ditch by a railroad track.

During the first three days you were gone, I imagined hundreds of ways in which you might have been killed. I have never been more hurt or tormented in my life. Once we heard you were all right, I became angry with you for all the pain you caused me. Your father and I talked of a number of ways to punish you, including having Sheriff Wilson lock you up as a runaway.

You must reflect on what you have done. You were gone for five days. No one here will speak to you for five days to give you time to think about what you did to us. You may come in the house only to sleep in your room, but you must use the back door. The rest of the time, you will stay in the barn. That is where you will study. I will set your food on the back porch, where you can get it and take it to the barn. You may wash outside, then go to your room after dark, but you are not to talk to Brooks, and he is not to talk to you. I have asked Miguel to take you to school and pick you up. I don't want you and Brooks riding together.

Momma

Ray stared at the road until Miguel turned down the hill toward the South Llano River. All of Ray's fears about tears were gone. His mother did not intend to speak to him. He wanted to rush inside, and tell her he was all right, that he was sorry; but Miguel pulled the truck to a stop by the barn. Slowly, Ray climbed out and walked into the barn. There was some hay piled in front of a horse stall. Ray plopped down on it, exhausted. A few tears trickled down his cheeks as he thought about how he had messed things up. In a few minutes, he was asleep in the hay. Ada placed his dinner on the back porch, as she said she would, but Ray didn't notice. The next thing Ray felt was a nudge from Miguel at daybreak. "I have your breakfast, *Señor* Ray," he said. Ray began rubbing his eyes and looked up at the gentle hog farmer he had known all his life. Steam was rising from the plate of eggs, sausage, and biscuits in Miguel's hand. During the night, Ada had covered her son with two warm blankets, and kissed his forehead, but Ray had not stirred. Even in the light, Ray could barely stay awake. He was exhausted from the journey.

The five days of punishment seemed endless. The kids at school wanted to know where Ray had been. He told them, but there was little enthusiasm in the stories as he recounted them to his friends. Ray was drained, and impatient to forget what had happened. His friends wanted to know whether he had been in jail, and most of his classmates seemed disappointed when they learned he hadn't. Ray was anxious as Miguel drove him home from Junction at the end of the fifth day. He would have to face his mother, and wondered if she would speak to him. Brooks was sitting on the front porch as the car pulled up. "Come on around to the barn," he said. Ray followed, considering whether his brother had been sent as an emissary from the family. Surprisingly, as Ray entered the barn, Brooks closed the door.

"What are you doing?" Ray questioned his older, but smaller brother. Brooks didn't answer, but instead hit Ray on the jaw, knocking him to the ground. "Get up!" Brooks commanded.

"What's the matter with you?" the dazed Ray protested.

"Get up!" Brooks ordered sternly. Like all brothers, Brooks and Ray had fought. Brooks had always been faster, and most of their lives, Ray had been bigger. Now, there was a hard seriousness glowering on Brooks' face that Ray had never seen before. Ray tried to grab his brother to stop the fight. Then he tried to wrestle Brooks to the ground, but Brooks moved like lightning, striking the bigger Oakley brother at will. Brooks' jabs felt like kicks from a mule.

The fight was no contest. Brooks carefully avoided Ray's nose, mouth, and eyes, so that Ray would not be badly marked by the beating he was taking. Repeatedly, Brooks would stun Ray with a sharp jab to the chin or jaw, then move in and pound his rib cage. After three attacks and knockdowns, Ray's torso was so sore he was ready to beg Brooks to stop, something he never remembered having done with anyone. As Ray's head slumped forward, a powerful uppercut from Brooks' right hand knocked Ray into unconsciousness, and he fell to the ground. Twenty minutes later, Ray opened his eyes to see Brooks staring at him. Brooks was seated on a bale of hay across the barn. His face was angry. After a few minutes, Ray was able to speak.

"What did you do that for?" he asked. Brooks glared at his younger brother.

"Don't ever do anything like that to our mother again," he ordered. Brooks stood, walked to the door, opened it, and walked across the yard into the house.

Walter always offered the same prayer at every meal, but on that particular evening he added a line of thanks for the safe return of his son. The atmosphere at dinner was stilted. Edythe and Ruth had lots of questions they were dying to have answered, but Ada's steely, commanding posture and facial expression made absolutely clear to everyone that she would not tolerate the kind of chatter the girls had in mind. When supper was finished, and the girls began clearing the table, Walter motioned to Ray.

"Come on out to the porch," he said. When they were outside in the cool night air, Walter spoke quietly. His voice cracked slightly as he began. "I see Brooks already gave you a pretty good beating. He shouldn't have done it, but it saved you the strapping I was going to give you," Walter said.

There was a period of silence. "If you intend to throw your life away the way that Glenn did, you've made a pretty good start," Ray's father announced forlornly. Ray braced himself for a lengthy sermon. He wanted to protest, but he knew he deserved whatever was coming. So he set himself for an interminable barrage of harsh rhetoric, but that was not Walter's way. He walked over to the porch rail and looked out into the yard for more than a minute, then stepped down to the ground and walked toward the river, leaving Ray standing in the chilly night alone. None of this had been like Ray had imagined during his long ride home on the train. A few minutes after Walter had disappeared into the darkness, Ray went into the house. His mother sat reading her Bible in the living room.

"Mother, I'm sorry," Ray sobbed as he stared across the room at Ada. His mother looked up from her reading.

"It's not that easy, Ray," she said. Ray stood with the tears wetting his cheeks, and waited for her to say something else, but Ada went back to her scripture, and did not look at her son again. Ray waited through the silence for a few minutes, then climbed the stairs to his room. Brooks was already in bed. Ray undressed and crawled into his bed. The comfortable mattress, and the clean sheets felt good, but Ray could not sleep. It was after midnight when he finally drifted off.

As spring progressed, Ray kept to himself. His grades were good, but that was the only aspect of Ray's life where Ada expressed pleasure. Ray went to spring football practice, and performed as well as ever, but something was fundamentally different. For the first time in his life, Ray didn't feel comfortable with Brooks. It seemed to Ray that Brooks watched him with a suspicious eye. Walter approached Ray several times, but their conversations never gained any traction.

The day after school ended for the summer, while the rest of the family was asleep, Ray slipped out of the house, picked up a bedroll he had packed with extra clothes, and a few other things and walked from the barn up the hill to the road. Ada had awakened at first light and gone to her window just in time to see Ray moving up the hill carrying a bedroll. She knew where he was going, and Ray's mother began crying quietly.

CHAPTER TWELVE

Ray caught a ride with the Oakleys' neighbor Kenneth Muenich.

"Going somewhere, Ray?" Mr. Muenich asked.

"Yes sir, I'm going to visit my uncles in New Mexico," Ray lied.

"Seems like I remember hearing that your pa was from New Mexico," Mr. Muenich continued. "Hope it's not as hot there as it is here. I don't know whether the corn is going to make this year or not. Certainly won't if we don't get some rain soon," the neighbor observed.

"Yes sir," Ray agreed. In about fifteen minutes Mr. Muenich let Ray out at the depot.

"I guess you'll have a little wait for the seven-twenty," he said. "How come your folks didn't come down to send you off? New Mexico's a far piece," Mr. Muenich added.

"Mother wasn't feeling well, and Dad didn't want to leave her. Since it was so early, I didn't want to wake Brooks up. I was pretty sure there would be plenty of cars going to town on Saturday," Ray explained dishonestly.

"Well I hope your ma gets to feeling better, and I hope you have a good visit with your folks," Mr. Muenich told his young neighbor.

"Thanks for the ride, Mr. Muenich," Ray called before waving goodbye. Ray turned and began walking toward the railway station as Mr. Muenich slipped his truck into gear and drove toward the store. Ray paused, waiting for him to pass out of sight before crossing to the side of the road opposite the station and walking east, where a freight train sat taking on water. Ray was casual as he walked toward the middle of the train, spotted an open door on a boxcar and vaulted up and into the empty car. There were no railroad detectives in Junction. And even if a train crewman had spotted Ray, it is unlikely they would have bothered him. Sheriff Wilson didn't allow transients to stay overnight in Junction, so the train crews never looked for them there. In a few minutes, the Southern Pacific freight blasted its whistle, and Ray started his long ride to California, this time as an experienced traveler. He had extra clothes and a blanket. He knew how to avoid the detectives, and he felt confident that he would be in California in a few days.

Kenneth Muenich spent most of the day in Junction. On his way home, he decided to stop by the Oakleys' to see if Ada was feeling better. She answered the door in her apron. Her face looked pale, and her eyes were red.

"Are you feeling better, Mrs. Oakley?" Mr. Muenich asked, as Ada opened the screen, allowing her unexpected guest to enter.

"No," Ada answered vacantly, then thought for a minute. "Who told you I was feeling bad?" she inquired.

"Why Ray, when I took him to the train this morning," he answered. Ada had known all day that Ray had caught a train for California. She had been anticipating all spring that her younger son would make another attempt. Ray had not left a note this time as he had done previously. Ray and Ada had barely spoken since his return to Telegraph, so it didn't seem likely that he could write what he could not speak. Ray hoped his mother would understand that he just had to do what he was doing.

Knowing Ray would run away again did not help Ada understand at all why her son was doing this to his mother. She had been crying all day. Ada was broken hearted, and feared that Ray would wind up dead, just as Glenn had. She had been attempting to convince herself that

Ray would not be hurt or killed, at least not on this particular trip. Ada wiped a tear from the corner of her eye with her apron.

"Then you saw him get on the train?" Ada asked Mr. Muenich.

"No, I dropped him at the depot, but I'm sure he got on the train to New Mexico all right. He had over an hour," Mr. Muenich explained.

"New Mexico?" Ada blurted out.

"Yes, to see Walter's brother. He does live in New Mexico, doesn't he?" Mr. Muenich asked.

"One of them still does, yes. The rest moved to Fort Worth," Ada offered weakly. Ray had so little interest in this distant part of his family, he hadn't known about the moves to Fort Worth. Ray probably couldn't have even gotten the names correctly and had even less knowledge of his father's sisters.

"Well is there anything the missus can bring you? Some soup maybe?" Mr. Muenich asked.

"No, thank you, Mr. Muenich," Ada replied. "I took some medicine, and I'm sure I'll be better in the morning." Ada never lied, not even about such a small thing as taking castor oil when she had not, but it was the only thing she could think of to get Mr. Muenich out of her living room.

"Well, I hope you get to feeling better soon," Mr. Muenich concluded.

"I'm sure I'll be as good as new tomorrow," Ada predicted, as she walked toward the door. Kenneth Muenich placed his felt hat back on his bald head as soon as he was outside.

"Thanks for taking Ray to the train," Ada called to her neighbor as he stepped off the porch. "And thanks for checking on me." Mr. Muenich waved to his neighbor.

"No trouble at all. Goodbye," he called.

"Goodbye," Ada responded.

As soon as the door closed, Ada called upstairs to Walter. She sent him into Junction to wire Ike, asking him to look out for Ray. Ada and Walter both knew Ray wasn't going to New Mexico for a family visit, but they felt better making some kind of effort. While he was at the station, Walter asked the agent to check the drawer just to make sure a ticket had not been written for Ray. No one had boarded the 7:20 in Junction that morning.

As the freight rolled through southwest Texas, Ray was struck by how different things were from his first ride. It was hot, even with the doors on the boxcar wide open. A blistering, dusty wind blew up from the Chihuahuan Desert in Mexico. The further west he rode, the more barren the landscape became. Late in the afternoon, the train crossed the massive bridge over the Pecos River. Ray recalled his early childhood, listening as his father talked with some men about how they had built that bridge. Walter had been almost as young as Ray was now when he had worked on the bridge across the Pecos. That was hard for Ray to imagine. Because to Ray, Walter had always been an old man, a man from a long-ago era. As Ray looked at the bridge, and the desert around it, he realized he was right. His father was a man from another time—a time when the west was opening up to receive the overflow from the east, which in turn was spilling out its surplus of immigrants from Europe. Walter was a man of nineteenth century America, when anything was possible—a time when dreams and hard work overcame the stifling harshness of frontier Texas. Hard work seemed endless on Walter's frontier, but enduring the hardships had led to success, comfort, and even relative wealth for Walter, and a select few Texans of his generation.

As Ray looked around, he thought of what he had seen and read about twentieth century men who were willing to work just as hard for their dreams. Often for so many, the twentieth century American dream was survival—hope of finding enough for the kids to eat for the night, dreaming of a place to stay out of the weather for one more night. For these desperate Americans, Ray came to believe that hope for prosperity had faded, then vanished. California was the only dream left for young Ray Oakley's fellow countrymen, many of whom were only a little older than Ray. Their jobs were gone. Their homes were gone. Their farms were gone. And if things didn't work out for them in California, the faint glimmer of their last chance dreams would be gone too. Why had life been so simple for Walter, and why had living become so impossibly complex now, Ray wondered?

Ray should have been asking himself why he seemed to identify with the Okies he was chasing to California. That there was irony in the emotional connection he had made in his mind with these less fortunate people never occurred to Ray. The Oakleys still had their farm, and money in the bank, a strong local bank that had not failed. They could ride a passenger train into San Antonio anytime they wanted, stay in a hotel, and eat food in fancy restaurants. Walter owned a new car, and there was an old Ford that Brooks drove the other kids to school in. When someone was sick, the doctor came to the house and was paid in cash. However, in Ray's mind, he was somehow not part of these things. Maybe that's why he was chasing after the pictures of hardship he had seen in the magazines—chasing these feelings all the way to California.

In truth, Ray didn't know why he was doing what he was doing. He didn't understand that he apparently lacked the capacity to be still. No one in Ray's youth had ever heard of ADHD. All he knew was that he just had to go. As the train chugged toward El Paso through the furnace-like heat of the early Texas summer, Ray also recalled his parents' warnings that he was on a path to an early, tragic death like the one Glenn had found. He knew they were trying to scare him back to his senses. He knew also that they were speaking from the overwhelming grief that Glenn had left behind, but Ray was far from certain that there was any truth to their warnings. Because he knew so little about Glenn, Ray tried to find out if he was really like his older brother. He had talked with Brooks about it, but Brooks really didn't know any more about Glenn than Ray did. One time when Maryon was home, he decided to ask her, but she wouldn't talk about her dead brother. It was too painful for her. Ralph had moved to San Antonio, and hardly ever came back to Telegraph. But Ray didn't believe anything his oldest brother said, anyway. One thing Ray knew about Glenn was that he liked to get drunk and stayed that way most of the time. Ray had tried drinking with some of his friends in Junction. He liked it, liked the way it made him feel, but he didn't stay drunk. Perhaps he had not had enough experience drinking to want to stay drunk all the time? Maybe he should not drink anymore so he wouldn't risk becoming like Glenn? However, from what Ray had heard, Glenn didn't like anything but drinking, and Ray was certainly not like that. Ray liked new things, excitement. He liked to travel. No, he had to travel. He wasn't running away. He was just going to see things. So, Ray wasn't at all like Glenn, he decided.

Well, he was like Glenn in one way. When Ray left, it made Ada hurt miserably. He knew that, and he didn't want to hurt his mother. If only she could understand that he had to do what he was doing. He had stayed in Telegraph all spring to finish the school year for her, even though every day a magnetic force had seemed to be pulling him toward the railroad tracks. Maybe he could write her a letter and explain to her why he had to travel, why he was not like her dead son. He'd think about that more later. One thing Ray knew about his parents. They seemed to have their minds made up about most things. They thought life was pretty much as it should be. Ray wanted almost nothing of what they had in their lives. He wanted adventure, and he wanted a new and different world. He was on his way to find it, and he knew they were going to stay in the world they liked. Walter and Ada would never want to hear an explanation that went the way Ray was thinking of trying to explain things to his parents.

Ray decided he needed to shake those thoughts out of his head. Those were problems he couldn't solve. He shifted his attention to California, and what he would find when he got there. But even California couldn't hold Ray's attention in the intense Texas heat. He drifted off into a hazy sleep. Ray opened his heavy eyes and saw the countryside passing by from time to time, leaving him only vaguely aware of the thoughts running randomly through his mind. Mostly his head was occupied by nondescript dreams, and Ray didn't become fully alert again until nearly sunset.

CHAPTER THIRTEEN

The temperature began to drop quickly after the sun went down. It wasn't cold, just cool enough to feel pleasant. One thing Ray had learned from his first experience riding freight trains was not to fall asleep and ride into a big city rail yard where the detectives prowled. On his first trip, Ray had money, but not this time. Walter and Ada had hoped that depriving Ray of money would help keep him home. Ray caught the train carrying two dollars and some change in his pocket. One important item he had brought on this trip that he had lacked on his first ride was a map, which he had borrowed from a book in the school library. It had grown too dark to read the map, but Ray had been studying it for several days. He vaguely remembered that there were at least two towns between the Pecos River Bridge and El Paso. So when the train rolled to a stop in Alpine, Ray dropped to the ground and began walking inconspicuously back toward the east. Less than a mile from the station, Ray came upon a trestle over a dry wash, located a sheltered area close to the timbers supporting the structure, unrolled his blankets and fell asleep.

The next morning, he woke with the sun, straightened himself out and walked to the highway. He wanted to avoid walking along the tracks. By carrying a bedroll over his shoulder, it was obvious that Ray was a transient. He immediately attracted the attention of the deputy sheriff, who was having an early morning look around Alpine. The deputy did not stop Ray but made several passes along the highway to make certain Ray kept moving through the town without stopping. After he had cleared the western city limits of Alpine, Ray found a curve where he calculated a train would have to slow down and waited there. He had brought some leftover biscuits and cornbread from his mother's kitchen. Having saved them as long as he could, Ray gobbled the dry bread quickly. He had also brought one bottle of Coca-Cola, the only liquid he could conveniently carry.

    He looked at the Coke and realized that it would have been smarter to have borrowed one of Walter's canteens that hung in the barn near the saddles. It was too late for that now. Ray used his pocketknife to pry the top off the soft drink. He consumed the hot soda in three giant gulps, dropped the bottle on the ground, and considered again how much smarter it would have been to bring a canteen. With nothing more to eat and nothing left to drink, Ray began to consider where and how he might get his next meal; but those speculations were cut short by the whistle of a slow freight pulling out of the station in Alpine. With no cover available, Ray lay flat on the ground as he waited for the train. But his attempt at stealth fooled no one. The train crew laughed and waved as the locomotive passed Ray, so he stood up and began looking for an open door. The train was moving just over five miles an hour as it started up the grade. This time, boarding was painless. Because Ray had been spotted, he knew he would have to drop off the train before it rolled into Marfa, but that couldn't be helped. There had just not been any place to hide. Ray lost over an hour in Marfa, because the train had moved through town before he could catch up. He had the same problem in Van Horn, so it was mid-afternoon when the young traveler arrived in El Paso. Ray jumped off as the train slowed for the yard. He was amazed that El Paso was such a big city and even more surprised to discover that almost every face he passed was brown. Other than the Velasquez family, Ray had known few Tejanos. The naive teen felt like he was in Mexico, an exciting notion, because it meant Ray's adventure was finally under way. He knew this would be his only chance to eat for the rest of the day, so he went looking for a tamale cart, remembering how good the spicy Mexican food had tasted in Austin. Ray started to buy a dozen. However, the old peddler, sensing Ray was a young man on the road with little money, gave Ray only half a dozen. From the under part of his cart, the old man produced a dozen corn tortillas. "Only two cents," he explained to Ray. "And they will fill you up. Save some for later," the old man advised.

Ray gulped down an orange Nehi soda with his tamales and put a second bottle in his bedroll for later. Ray thought once more how much better off he would be, if he had brought a canteen. El Paso was so fascinating that Ray became caught up in sightseeing, and lost track of time. He decided to walk across the bridge into Mexico. However, when he was a block from the bridge, he noticed the sun was beginning to set. Ray changed his mind, concluding that it might be smarter to catch a train before dark. So keeping to the pattern he had established earlier, he worked his way back to the tracks and followed along them toward the west until he was out of town. In a few minutes, he heard a freight rounding the bend toward him. Ray had to run as hard as he could to catch up with the open car he had selected. For the first time on this trip, Ray got splinters in his hands when he jumped on board. He did not, however, tear the knees out of his pants. He was making a little progress compiling his hoboing skills, Ray thought with a trace of self-satisfaction.

This freight train was different than any he had ever seen. It was made up entirely of empty icebox cars being returned to California for loads of fresh fruits and vegetables. Ray guessed there were a hundred cars on the train. But since they were all empty, the freight zipped along at passenger train speed. He wanted to jump before the train entered the yard in Las Cruces, but the engineer stayed on the main line and rolled right past the station at fifteen miles per hour. The empty freight train pulled by a giant locomotive picked up speed on the flat land west of Las Cruces and soon clicked along at sixty miles per hour. The engineer slowed to fifteen as he neared the depot in Deming but soon had the big Southern Pacific steam engine highballing for Arizona. Ray had made up all the time he had lost looking around El Paso and then some.

He had walked for hours in El Paso, and he was tired. Despite his best efforts, he fell asleep, and did not realize the train had pulled onto a siding in Lordsburg to let an eastbound passenger train pass until he felt a poke of a stick in his belly and heard a hoarse whisper. "Get up kid. Bulls is coming," the voice said. Ray rolled out of the car and onto the gravel of the ballast quickly. Experience had taught him not to wait for a second warning about the presence of railroad security men. The old man grabbed Ray's belt and pulled him under a car on an adjacent track. The detectives were just one car away, slipping quietly past the open reefer, shining their flashlights inside. They switched the lights off until they got to the next car.

Four cars behind the one where Ray had been riding, the security men pulled out three Mexican boys. Two were dragged out of the car. A third attempted to jump and landed right in the arms of a giant guard. Ax handles flew wildly, and the young men's shrieks pierced the New Mexico darkness. The words they yelled were in Spanish, so Ray could not understand. However, it was clear by what little could be seen, and from the boys' panicked cries, that they were taking a terrible beating. After a couple of minutes, the guards began dragging the boys across the rocks, dirt, and tracks. Their screams had lost some volume, but they continued to yell out in pain. As the distance between Ray and the old man and the three boys increased, the sounds faded.

"How did you know I was in there?" Ray whispered as a question to the old man.

"I heard you snoring," the old man answered.

Ray laughed quietly. "I guess for once that helped me out," Ray suggested.

"Yeah," the old man concurred. "But if you're going to ride these trains, you gotta learn when and where to sleep, or you'll wind up dead."

The smile disappeared from Ray's face. "I know," Ray agreed. "I didn't intend to fall asleep. I guess I just got too tired in El Paso today. I made a rule for myself not to fall asleep between towns. Where am I, anyway?

"Lordsburg," the old man answered.

"Well, I guess that's part of the problem," Ray said. "That guy just highballed through the last two towns."

The old man nodded slightly to indicate his agreement, "Yeah, they'll fool you all right," he remarked, "But if you're going to survive out here, you have to learn when to stay awake. You just have to," he added for emphasis. "I'm the Farmer," the old man announced, extending his hand.

"Ray, Ray Oakley," adding his last name as a sign of trust and gratitude, remembering that the old man had just saved him from a terrible beating or worse.

"Good to meet you Ray," the old man smiled. "You an experienced 'bo?" he asked, knowing that Ray was not.

"No sir," Ray answered respectfully. "This is only my second trip."

The man offered another affirming nod "Well, you'll learn. But you can't fall asleep like that.

"You got anything to eat?" the Farmer asked.

Ray began fumbling through his stuff, amazed that he had remembered to drag it off the train with him. In a few seconds, he fished out the tortillas, producing a small laugh from his new traveling companion

"No, I wasn't asking you for food. I wanted to know if you needed something to eat. Put those tortillas up. They'll come in handy later," the Farmer smiled, handing Ray a strip of jerky. "Try some of this. I think you'll like it," he added, still displaying a disarming smile. Ray took the offered strip of dried meat from the old man, struggled to bite some off, then labored harder to chew. The meat tasted good, but it took Ray a while to eat it all. Halfway through, the old man gave Ray a hard biscuit to go with the jerky. "Can't really eat stuff like this, when you start losing your teeth," the Farmer laughed.

Ray would have laughed, but he was straining with the challenging new food. After Ray had finished the meal, he began fishing through his blankets for the orange drink he had saved from El Paso. He found the bottle, worked the top off with his knife, and started to take a big drink. Just as Ray raised the bottle to his lips, he stopped and offered it to the old man first.

"Thanks, son," the old man chuckled. "Never touch the stuff. I used to drink beer and whiskey, but I'm too old for that. Now I only drink spring water, and sometimes a little buttermilk. You go ahead, though" the Farmer said, gesturing for Ray to drink up. Ray downed the Nehi in three swallows.

When Ray had finished his drink, there was a period of quiet before the old man spoke. "Come on. I'll show you where we sleep," the Farmer offered. Ray held back. "It's all right," the old man laughed. "I won't bother you. I'm too old, even if I was of a mind that way," the Farmer explained, continuing to laugh. Ray felt uncomfortable, awkward, because the old man had detected his hesitancy. But Ray followed the Farmer three- or four-hundred yards to a trestle just outside the yard. As they walked underneath the small bridge and into the dry creek bed, Ray saw there was a smoldering mesquite fire. Five men lay in bedrolls eight or ten feet away from the fire. "They're all right," the old man assured Ray, who was still wondering what he was getting himself into. "I've been with all these boys for a long time, but you're right to be cautious. Can't ever tell who you'll run into on the road. More good than bad out here, though," the Farmer offered. "Not many real crooks and bandits ride the rails. Most of us don't have enough to steal," the old man added with another flourish of laughter.

"Put your stuff over there," he directed Ray, pointing to a spot away from the others. "Don't need to worry about the cold this evening. The blankets'll take care of us without keeping up a fire all night," he instructed. Ray, who seldom felt cold, guessed the old man was right; but the air in the desert was a good deal cooler than he was used to at home along the South Llano River. Ray followed the old man's directions, spread out his blankets and lay down, his head cluttered with the thoughts of the eventful day behind him. The old man stirred the fire back to life, then retreated a few steps to watch it burn. Ray eyed him for a minute or two before falling asleep.

CHAPTER FOURTEEN

Around six o'clock, Ray woke to the inviting smells from a mesquite fire and brewing coffee. He rose and walked toward the campfire rubbing sleep from his eyes. The old man handed Ray a cup of coffee.

"What are your plans for the day?" the old man asked, displaying a cheerful smile—even at six a.m.

"I'm going to California," Ray replied, still more asleep than awake.

"What's out there?" the old man continued. "I just want to see what's going on," Ray responded. He didn't like being questioned about his intentions, motives or much of anything else, but the old man was kind and disarming, and he had saved Ray from the detectives.

"Well, there's lots of bulls out there. They stop all the trains to get all the Okies and bums off," the old man resumed. "Most people get a beating first thing in. Groups with women and kids, they make them go into the camps. Men and boys without families, they put them on the work gangs or beat 'em until they decide to go back to where they came from. Is that what you'd heard was going on out there?" the Farmer queried in an even voice, his smile undiminished.

Ray could not keep the look of shock from his face, but he did restrain himself from blurting out his surprise. "That seems like a lot of trouble for the railroads to go to just to keep people from riding the trains," Ray said finally after a period of silence, hoping to show the old man he wasn't ready to believe just anything he heard.

"Oh, it's not just the railroads. Most of the bulls in California now is lawmen, deputies and the like. Some places, townsfolk are patrolling in bunches with shotguns rounding up the Okies and taking them to the camps themselves. For a time, the growers wanted them in. The more of 'em that came, the lower the price of picking the fruit and working the fields got.

"But after a while, the Okies began to overrun everything. They started camping in the parks and the fields, and even on the streets. People in California had enough, and the bulls were called in to put a stop to it. Some places, they're even talking about calling up troops to clear out the Hoovervilles," the old man said, his smile still uncracked, and his voice indicating that he and Ray were just having an ordinary conversation the way old friends would. Ray fell silent for a longer period. He had to concede that the old man seemed to know what he was talking about. But the Farmer was giving Ray a lecture with a warning included. And even though it was delivered gently, Ray didn't like any form of admonition. He wasn't used to it and had no intention of placidly enduring a corrective lesson. Concurrently, there was a deeper problem for Ray. If California had really been transformed into a police state, then the Farmer was telling Ray that his trip had all been for nothing, an eventuality that Ray just wasn't prepared to accept.

"You ain't no Okie," the old man observed. "What's in California for you?"

Ray, now unable to conceal the agitation in his voice, challenged the Farmer.

"How do you know I'm not an Okie?"

Keeping his tone light and friendly, the old man explained. "Clothes. Them clothes is almost new. Okie boy your age wouldn't have had any new clothes in two years. May not have had any in his whole life," the Farmer explained. Again the conversation paused for a significant time.

"Maybe things are better in California now than they were when you were out there," Ray suggested, hinting at hope.

"I doubt it. I just come back two days ago," the old man said.

"Why didn't the bulls beat you?" Ray asked. "You don't look like you've been roughed up."

The old man answered simply. "I know how to stay away from 'em. And when I just have to be around bulls, I give 'em money." Seeing Ray was unconvinced, the Farmer reached into his pocket and pulled out a roll of one-hundred-dollar bills. He opened the money up and spread it in his hand. Ray saw that there were more than ten of the bills in the old man's hand. He couldn't count them precisely, because some bills covered others.

"So what's an old bum like me doing with all this money?" the Farmer laughed. Ray was speechless. "I'm a businessman, son. I just do my business in an unusual place," he explained, answering his own question. The old man was crazy. Ray was now sure of it.

"I appreciate the coffee," Ray declared. "And thanks for helping me out last night," Ray concluded, extending his arm to give the old man his cup back. The Farmer's laughter became so loud that it roused several of the sleeping men.

"Think I'm crazy, do you?" the old man managed, as his laughing stretched on. "Figure you better get away before I hit you in the head with an ax or something?" By now, several of the sleepy men were laughing as well. The Farmer didn't accept the cup Ray was offering, so Ray let it fall to the ground as he began backing away from the fire and toward his blankets. He kept an eye fixed on the old man as he walked.

The Farmer stopped laughing. "I'm not crazy, and I won't hurt you," he spoke, hoping to reassure the young visitor to his camp. "I'm sorry if I scared you. I was just trying to convince you that if you ride a train into California, you're likely to wind up either hurt, in jail, or both." Ray ceased walking backward. "I grow marijuana," the old man stated modestly. "I grow it all along the Southern Pacific right of way and I sell it in California. That's where I get all this money, and if you'd been riding these trains for more than a few days, you'd know that. Everybody out here knows about me. Lots of these boys work for me sometimes and I give 'em money when they need it." Ray stood in shocked silence, taking in what the old man had told him. When he looked up, the Farmer was scratching his head.

"Where you from, son?" the old man asked Ray.

"Texas," Ray answered. "I know that," the old man remarked. "What part?" he asked.

"Kimble County," Ray added quietly. "Then you must be kin to Walter Oakley," the Farmer supposed.

"Yes sir," Ray said.

"He your daddy or your uncle?"

Ray replied that Walter was his father.

"Then you got people not far from here," the old man suggested.

"Yes sir," Ray confirmed.

"Well, maybe you ought to drop in on them, and see how they're doing," the Farmer suggested.

"I don't really know them," Ray responded.

"Well, I think they're pretty good folks. I think they'd take you in," the old man said. Ray didn't answer, and the conversation paused again. "Then I guess you're not of a mind to do that," the old man concluded.

Ray didn't answer. He had become angry with his father, once again. Wasn't there anyone in Texas who didn't know Walter Oakley, Ray wondered? Then he remembered that he was no longer in Texas. He was almost to Arizona.

"How do you know my father?" Ray asked. His tone was testy.

"Well son, he practically built this railroad you been riding on—him and Mr. Easterly." The two lapsed into silence for a time. The Farmer allowed Ray a moment to absorb everything he had heard in the past few minutes. It was a lot for Ray to digest.

"If you're going to ride these trains, you got learning to do. Get some of those biscuits over there," the old man directed, pointing to a skillet on the ground close to the fire. "After breakfast, I guess I'll start in teaching school. I've got some crops to check on out west, anyway" he smiled. Ray and the Farmer rode freight trains through southern Arizona and New Mexico for three days. Ray helped the Farmer tend his crops. Amazingly, the illegal plants could not be seen from the train, but the Farmer knew where each patch was. He knew which ones needed water, and which ones were ready for harvest. Several times during the journey, a hobo seemed to mysteriously appear to help the old man with what he liked to call his farming. Ray helped with the watering; and twice when no one else was available, Ray, despite serious reservations, helped harvest the marijuana.

The example of Glenn's excessive drinking had little negative consequence on Ray's behavior, at least to this point in his young life. But Ray strongly believed that drugs, opium Ray had been told, had played a major role in his older brother's tragic death. Even though Ray knew almost nothing about marijuana, he was opposed to the use of all kinds of drugs, because of the awful things he had heard about his dead brother's actions when he was under the influence of the strong narcotic. The Farmer answered that he only sold his product to people who wanted it. Even though the Farmer said the plant was relatively harmless, he told Ray he never used what he grew. The Farmer also limited his contact with the people who actually used the drugs he sold them. The transients who made up the Farmer's entourage, and helped with tending the plants were eased out of his circle, if they became regular users of the drug. He didn't want anyone who stayed under the influence in his close circle regarding users as irresponsible. At the end of their trip together, the Farmer gave Ray five dollars for helping.

"The lesson was worth a lot more than the money," the Farmer had explained. Ray absolutely knew he was entwining himself in a risky situation, but he liked the old man. That was one of Ray's failings. He knew the Farmer was a criminal, but Ray had been captivated by the Farmer's charm. Where the old man was concerned, Ray saw only what he wanted to see, while knowingly blinding himself to the aspects of the Farmer's activities which Ray knew to be illegal, perilous, and just plain wrong.

"Son, you'd still be a lot better off going down to stay with your daddy's folks than riding into California on a freight train," the old man warned.

"Maybe so, but I've got to finish what I came to do." Ray explained.

"Good luck then," the Farmer pronounced.

"Thanks, and thanks for the schooling," Ray responded.

"I hope you learned enough to keep you alive," the Farmer concluded with a grin. But Ray could not possibly have missed seeing the concern on the old man's face when they parted.

CHAPTER FIFTEEN

Ray camped in the hobo jungles in Tucson and Phoenix just the way the Farmer had instructed, and the young traveler had been immediately accepted every time. Ray never failed to introduce himself as the Farmer's friend and pupil. The food was basic, but there was plenty, enough to fill up even Ray. In Tucson, he had left a sack of potatoes behind, and he had contributed a sack of flour in Phoenix to pay for his keep, following the ways the Farmer had drilled into him. Ray had bought the food, rather than stolen it—even though he had to walk some distance in both cities to reach a store. Ray thumbed his nose at other people's rules, and he was in no way perfect. But thievery was something he detested. Of course, he had also made a rule for himself to avoid everything associated with illegal drugs. But he had broken his own rule about drugs for two reasons. He wanted to learn what the Farmer could teach him about life on the road. Ray genuinely admired the old man. The Farmer had told Ray to give food rather than money. Before leaving Phoenix, Ray applied another of the Farmer's lessons, going to a boarding house and paying a quarter to take a bath and shave. He dressed in his clean clothes and hopped a westbound freight. At a spot two miles east of Yuma, where the train slowed to a crawl, again acting just as the Farmer had told him it would, Ray left the train without injury, and without getting his clothes covered with dust. He managed to hitch a ride with a salesman, offering him fifty cents for a lift to the bus depot in El Centro. The salesman refused the money, but he had taken Ray directly to the bus station.

The Farmer's prediction had proved accurate. The freshly clean Ray and the salesman sailed right through the sheriff's checkpoint at the California state line, a place with a huge swarm of people. It was far more crowded than a border crossing into Mexico, and more squalid as well. The road was lined with Okies in their old farm trucks loaded above the height of the cab with furniture and belongings, all held in place by ropes and wires. Most of the mass of displaced people were being turned away by California authorities. The unsuccessful entrants were told they could not cross into California because they could not prove they had a job or family waiting. Inside California, commissioned lawmen, deputized townspeople, and representatives of the Salvation Army were easy to pick out. They looked like speckles among the horde of people hoping to rebuild shattered lives by the place they had been promised was a paradise beside the Pacific. Ray was fascinated, but the misery surrounding him nearly caused him to throw up. He got out of the salesman's car in front of the bus station in El Centro, thanked the man, waved goodbye, and walked to the window to buy a ticket.

"Hour before the next bus to Los Angeles. Catch it right over there," the agent informed Ray, pointing to a door with a sign marked buses over it. The attendant passed Ray's ticket and change to him through the window and called for the next customer to step forward. Ray noted a city police officer moving through the crowd in the bus station looking for people who did not have tickets. To escape the stifling heat in the crowded terminal, Ray walked outside to a covered porch. Across the street, Ray spotted a stand selling the most dazzling assortment of fresh fruits he had ever seen. It overflowed with peaches, plums, oranges, grapes, and an exotic fruit the Chicano vendor called a nectarine. Ray gave the man a dime and received a paper sack and was instructed to choose a half-dozen pieces of fruit. As Ray turned back toward the bus station, he was mobbed by hungry ragged, Okie children, all of them weak from lack of food. He could sense the children's pain as he looked into their hunger-glazed eyes. Eating the fruit was out of the question. Ray smiled as he handed the bag to one of the older children, then watched as they retreated a block away to the shade of an ash tree to divide up the fruit Ray had brought. The Farmer had not been exaggerating. Conditions in California were horrible.

In an hour or so, the bus was speeding Ray away from the suffering and on to Los Angeles. At first, Ray could see only desert. Next, the bus passed through beautiful ranch lands. Then, suddenly, the coach was filled with lusciously cool air, blowing through the open windows. The cool breeze passing through the orange groves which stretched as far as he could see, had to be coming from the Pacific Ocean, Ray concluded as he read a sign that said Santa Ana, eight miles. The bus made a rest stop in Santa Ana, where Ray drank an orange soda. He walked through the open doorway and into the glorious weather outside the little bus station, marveling at how cool it felt as he stood in full sunshine. In Texas from the beginning of May through the end of September, people sought shade the instant they passed outdoors. But in Orange County California, shade seemed unnecessary, even in the brightest, fullest sunlight.

In just under an hour, Ray stepped off the bus in downtown Los Angeles, where he was immediately inundated, and perhaps endangered by a discordance of buses, streetcars, and taxis. He drew a deep breath and looked up to the forest of tall buildings rising into the sky. The structures were like others he had seen in San Antonio and El Paso—but in greater numbers. A pleasant breeze cooled a mesmerized Ray as he walked a few blocks to a park framed by palm trees that soared straight up into the unique blue sky that seemed to exist only in California. This was the place Ray had been dreaming about. He wasn't a young man prone to using superlatives, but he admitted to himself that he didn't know enough rhapsodic language to describe what he was seeing. The men wore prosperous, light colored, tropical suits, and the streets bustled, boasting that everything in California was growing and moving up. The Depression was close by, but the peddlers and panhandlers on the street corners provided the only evidence of America's hard times among the palm dotted streets of downtown L.A. Ray walked around for an hour, in awe of this shiny new city before it was time to look for the streetcar the Farmer had described, the one that would take him to the jungle. He found the line and remembered just before boarding a car to buy some potatoes to take along.

The camp where the hoboes were gathered was only a mile walk from the streetcar stop. Ray cheerfully approached a man cooking stew, introduced himself as a friend of the Farmer's, and was welcomed. While supper cooked, Ray lay around listening to the men tell stories. The young wanderer had quickly learned to feel at home in these camps with all the others who traveled on the cheap. He slept well. And the next day, Ray rode a streetcar to Santa Monica to see the ocean for the first time. He strolled out along the elaborate pier as the surf rolled onto shore. Ray found a concrete bench in a park overlooking the Pacific, where he just sat staring at the incredible blue water and watching giant waves crash onto the beach. He badly wanted to swim in the Pacific, but all the people on the beach had what the signs in the shop windows called bathing suits. Ray might have had enough money to buy one, but that would have left him broke. So he watched the big ocean pound the land.

At noon, he rode the streetcar along Santa Monica Boulevard into Hollywood, found a diner on Vine Street, and ate a bowl of chili for a nickel. He paid two more cents for an orange drink. Crackers came with the chili. After lunch, Ray walked by the movie studios. If he passed any stars, he didn't recognize them. He and Brooks only went to cowboy shows, and Ray knew that he had not seen Tom Mix, the young Texans' favorite actor. He climbed aboard a streetcar on Melrose, and rode over the hill into the Valley, a quaint mixture of small-town buildings and Spanish architecture bordered by vast orchards of oranges, grapefruit, and lemons that appeared to go on forever. As the sun began to set, Ray reluctantly took the streetcar back to the jungle. He spent the next three days exploring Los Angeles, sightseeing until his money was almost gone. One of the men in the encampment took Ray to a restaurant where Ray got a job washing dishes and scrubbing floors. It was hard work, ten hours a day. But at the end of six days, Ray had nine dollars for his trip to San Francisco.

The young man from Texas was having the time of his life and thoroughly enjoying his independence. Ray wasn't so busy that he couldn't easily have mailed his mother a postcard to let her know he was safe, but that just wasn't Ray's way. Not once did his parents' worries enter his thoughts. Ray was wholly focused on his own experiences and wrapped up in the stories of his new friends from the rails.

CHAPTER SIXTEEN

Ray was shocked and unprepared when railroad detectives and deputies surrounded his train as it stood idle on a siding five miles south of Salinas. The freight train was packed with Okies, Chicanos, and Braceros up from Mexico looking for work in the fields. In addition to Ray, seven people filled the empty reefer in which Ray rode, including five members of a family from Nebraska. Many of the travelers tried to run, when they heard the screamed commands from the lawmen and the beating of ax handles and bats against the sides of the cars. Experience had already taught Ray that most of those who ran got hurt. Anyway, he wasn't a runner. Ray was quickly handcuffed and taken to a circle of police cars half a mile from the train. He didn't resist, and he suppressed the urge to talk back to the deputies. As Ray sat cross legged in a circle, he managed to whisper to a California Highway Patrolman, who watched over the prisoners. The man walked over to confirm what Ray was saying, and Ray repeated his words. "If you cut me loose, I have some money," Ray whispered a second time.

"Why don't I just take the money out of your pocket and slap your head with this?" the patrolman answered in a low voice, gesturing with the weighted leather sap in his hand.

"Because I don't think you're a bad person," Ray answered, amazed at his own restraint, and surprised by the calm attempt he was making to appeal to the officer. The patrolman was silent for a moment, and Ray's intuition gave him hope that the patrolman was not genuinely committed to his official mission—beating Okies to the edge of death. "I think you're tired of beating up poor people," Ray added. "And besides, I'm not looking for farm work. I was just riding a freight train to San Francisco." The man let Ray go but kept all of his nine dollars.

"He's from Berkeley," the corrupt, but apparently unsadistic, cop lied to his suspicious lieutenant. "He was just trying to get home by riding on a freight train." Ray listened to the highway patrolman's words, as Ray walked toward Highway 101. He encountered no other cops. All the lawmen were apparently tied up with the hapless migrants they had forced off the train. No one along the highway would stop to offer Ray a ride, so he walked all the way to Salinas. It was after midnight when Ray finally arrived at the jungle in San Francisco. Two very inebriated men were standing by the fire. To Ray's inexperienced eyes, the pair appeared to be drinking wine and probably had been at it all day. Ray gave the two drunks a wide berth and made his bed in a spot as far from the fire as he could while still remaining within the hobo encampment. Ray had no more money for robbers to take, but an attacker wouldn't know that. He awoke as soon as the camp began to stir. He rolled his blankets and moved toward the fire, where a cluster of early risers had gathered to drink coffee.

As Ray approached, a stocky man over six feet tall greeted him. "Square Jaw," the man said, extending his hand to Ray.

"I'm Ray Oakley," Ray responded, and shook the man's hand. Then he remembered to add: "I'm a friend of the Farmer's."

"Well, you'd be welcome even if you wasn't, son. We don't turn people away from here so long as they don't fight in camp or try to steal from the other men here. Looks like you were traveling pretty late last night.

"Ran into some bulls down near Salinas," Ray explained.

"Yeah," Square Jaw sympathized. "There's been a lot of problems down there. How'd you get away?"

Ray looked at his shoes. "I gave one of them all my money," he answered. This was big news, and the rest of the men around the fire wanted to hear everything that had happened. One of the men put a cup of coffee in Ray's hand while he told them the details. When he finished, Square Jaw spoke again.

"You want to find some work to get your stake back up?" he asked.

"Well, I need some money," Ray admitted, flashing a smile and letting out a chuckle. With two biscuits in his left hand, Ray was following one of the older men down the street only a couple of minutes later.

"We'll have to take the streetcar," the man told him. "We're pressed for time. Just about impossible to get hired if you show up late. My name's Josh, by the way," the man called as he led Ray onto the streetcar and dropped a coin into the box to pay Ray's fare. "You can pay me back tonight," he said. "They pay you every day at the cannery."

Fish odor permeated the moist air, as Ray and Josh walked down the hill to the wharf toward the enormous cannery. A mass of men milled about in front of the guard shack at the plant entrance. Josh guided Ray around the outside of the crowd and up to one of the three men who stood beside the hiring boss. The man recognized Josh right away. Josh whispered something in his ear. The man held out his hand and Josh slipped a half dollar into it. "I'll pay you back tonight," Ray promised Josh as the two men were ushered through the gate and into the plant. In less than a minute, Ray was given a timecard that he placed in the slot of a clock machine. He followed the crowd of men through another gate, onto a tuna boat, and down below into the hold of the ship. Except for a half hour break for lunch at eleven-thirty, Ray worked nonstop for eleven hours carrying the heavy fish up treacherously narrow ladders and out of the boat's holds. Ray lay down as the other men ate. They had brought lunches, but Ray had nothing to eat. Few of the men were as large as Ray. All were much older, and they couldn't afford to share their food. They needed all the food they possessed for their children at home. Fewer than thirty men worked on the crew unloading the big tuna boats. More than three hundred had been outside the gate that morning when Ray arrived. Most of them didn't know they needed to offer a bribe to get hired. Almost none of them had fifty cents in any event. So more than two hundred of them had gone away without work, meaning their children would not eat that day or night.

Exhausted after his grueling experience, Ray walked back to the camp that night. He was covered from head to toe with oil and blood from the stinking fish. Even if a streetcar conductor had allowed him on board, Ray was too embarrassed by the way he smelled to be around other people. When Ray arrived back at the jungle, there were a dozen or so men as dirty as he was from their day's work. Some were covered with the mortar and grime from construction jobs, some with oil and lubricants, and one with coal dust. No one else came close to matching Ray's level of stink. Unloading the tuna boats was the smelliest work around. One of the men Ray had met around the fire that morning led him to a corner of the camp underneath two rail trestles, where water was heated in four large garbage cans. There were makeshift showers, and a place to wash clothes. There was also a clothesline, which the friendly fella assured Ray was a safe place for his drying clothes to be left.

When Ray and his clothes were clean, he put on his spare clothes, which were still waiting where he had left them that morning. He located Josh and paid him the fifty-five cents he owed for his help that morning, leaving Ray with eighty-eight cents for the day's work.

"Thanks," Ray told Josh.

"Don't mention it," Josh responded. "Are you going back to work tomorrow?"

Ray sighed. "I guess I have to," he answered.

"Well, go around the side of the crowd like I showed you this morning," Josh directed. "You go see Curly again. He's the man I talked with. Curly knows you're with us now, so it'll be all right. You should only have to give him a quarter, tomorrow. Usually the four bits is only for Monday. But sometimes, when there aren't going to be enough boats for a full crew, the hiring bosses want more money. If you argue with them, even once, they won't ever hire you again. "And I didn't have time to tell you this morning. Never slack up when you're working. If you do, it makes the hiring boss look bad. They'll replace you on the spot and never hire you back. Do you understand?"

"Yes," Ray answered. "But tell me one thing. That was the hardest work I've ever done. How did you know I could do it?"

"Easy. I knew you had to," Josh replied with a smile. "Besides you're a big Texas farm boy, a lot bigger than most of those Italian and Irish men you were working with." Ray was amused. How come everybody knew he was from Texas without even asking? He laughed to himself, wondering if Josh knew his father, too. Everyone else he had met on his journey seemed to.

"Get over to the fire before all the stew's gone. Men that work aren't expected to scrounge for food, but you need to give Iron Jaw a quarter for your share of the food," Josh said.

Again, Ray missed the irony of what was going on around him. There were more rules in these camps than in his mother's kitchen, and at her dining table. The work was harder than any Ray had ever done on his father's farm, or at football practice. Most of the money Ray was earning wound up in someone else's pocket. Half-a-dozen times since Ray had been riding on freight trains, he had been arrested, almost arrested, or beaten by men with clubs. This information didn't take root in Ray's mind. All he could see was that he was free and having a grand adventure.

CHAPTER SEVENTEEN

The next morning, Ray was up at the first smell of coffee. He got a piece of bacon to go with the biscuits he had for breakfast, and the cook included two hard-boiled eggs to go along with the biscuits he had already wrapped in newspaper for Ray's lunch.

"I'd throw in a can of tuna fish for you to take along, but I don't think you'd be able to eat it dockside at the fish cannery," the cook teased. Everyone around the fire had a good laugh. Then Ray dashed off to catch the streetcar. Curly charged Ray seventy-five cents to work that day, even though nearly thirty men were hired again. Ray remembered Josh's advice just in time, resisting a compelling urge to backtalk Curly. His muscles were so sore he had trouble climbing into the hold the first time, provoking snickers from some of the men who were over forty years old. Ray sensed they resented he was working while older men with children were locked outside the gate, but no one said anything to Ray. As a matter of fact, the men all worked so hard that the only time there was any talk at all was during lunch. The second day Ray had thirty-eight cents left from his day's work after he paid Curly, bought his food and paid for the streetcar ride.

While he was bathing, Ray mused that Curly had made nearly twice as much from Ray's eleven hours of work as Ray had. And Curly had made his money without ever lifting a single fish. The young adventurer would have been angry except for the fact that he was just too tired. Was Ray really as sympathetic to the victims of the Depression as he had convinced himself when had been reading magazines and the newspapers in the school library in Junction? He was no longer reading magazine articles about the impoverished but living among them. Had Ray thought about what the children would eat that night, when he replaced one of the poor men on the wharf earlier in the day? No, Ray was too brain dead from his labors to wrestle with the intellectual inconsistencies of real life. He was so tired, that Josh had to wake him for work the next morning by nudging Ray with his toe.

"You going to work, son?" he asked. Ray's head bolted up, but the rest of his body hesitated. He was so stiff it took him almost thirty seconds to stand. "Don't go, if you can't finish the day," Josh cautioned.

"I'll be okay," Ray said, trying to convince himself as well as Josh. After Ray had stretched, he tried a question on Josh. "You know, in L.A. one of the men got me a job washing dishes and scrubbing floors. It was a lot easier than this, and paid better, too."

Josh offered an explanation, and a gentle warning as well. "Chinese do that work around here, and they work for almost nothing. Times are a lot tougher here than in L.A. Be grateful for what you got."

Ray said nothing else. In less than an hour, Ray was handing Curly another seventy-five cents. Ray saw that Curly was watching Ray's face carefully looking for a hint of complaint. Ray masked his anger with a blank facial expression as he passed through the gate. Climbing into the hold was even harder than it had been the day before, but Ray made sure that no sounds of pain escaped his mouth—even though his sore muscles forced him to move slowly down the steeply inclined steps.

By lunch, Ray had limbered up, and the body of the young football player had begun to show signs of adjusting to the back breaking conditions in the hold. He was working circles around the older men, and that caught the eye of the captain of the tuna boat he was unloading. When it was time for lunch, a mate on the boat had a whispered conversation with one of the hiring bosses, not Curly. The man walked over to Ray.

"Captain wants to see you," the hiring boss told Ray, pointing to the gray bearded man standing outside the ship's wheelhouse. Ray wanted to ask the hiring boss if he were in trouble, but instead he walked over to the captain in silence.

"You wanted to see me?" Ray posed, puzzled and suspicious.

"Smile boy. I won't bite you," the captain laughed.

"Yes sir," he complied, a smile creeping onto his face.

"One of my deckhands broke his arm. He won't be back for two-and-a-half weeks," the captain explained. "You ever been to sea?"

"No sir," Ray responded. "I'm from Texas."

The captain laughed, again. "Well, they got sailors in Texas, boy," he offered.

"Not in the Hill Country," Ray said.

"I've been watching you work," the captain observed. "I think you'll do, even if you don't know anything. I'll give you twenty dollars at the end of the two-and-a-half weeks, so you don't blow all your money. Your meals come with the job. You can sleep on the boat when we're in port, and of course you'll have to when we're at sea," the captain explained, laughing once more. Ray didn't say anything but looked down at the other men eating their lunch.

"I've already squared it with the hiring bosses, if that's what you're worried about. We'll sail in two hours, if you want to come," the captain offered with a smile.

"But if I leave before the end of the day, they'll never hire me again," Ray told the captain. "Do you really want to work here anymore?" the captain chuckled, and Ray laughed as well. That was the first thing anyone had said to him in several days that made sense.

"I'll get my stuff and be back in an hour-and-a-half," Ray said, beaming at the possibility of getting away from the wharf. Ray had gotten used to the odor that came from working with the fish and boarded the streetcar without thinking. The car was not crowded. So as Ray walked to the back, three or four passengers moved as far away from him as they could. When he saw the people change seats, Ray became embarrassed about the way he smelled. But if he was going to be back at the boat on time, Ray needed the speed of the streetcar. He said quick goodbyes to Square Jaw, Josh, and several others, thanking them for taking him in and promising he would see them again when his work at sea was finished. Ray didn't have time to bathe but changed into his clean clothes before heading back to the boat. Even Curly was friendly, as Ray passed through the yard and onto the *Pacific Lady*.

"Welcome aboard," Captain McDuff called to Ray. "Boris there will show you where to stow your gear" the captain said, pointing to his first mate. "Leave your dirty clothes out of the way on deck so your blankets don't smell like fish," the captain laughed. "You can wash them after we get out in open water."

The boat's crew was composed of the captain, first mate, another deckhand, and Ray. William, the other deckhand, gave Ray a big pole he called a gaff. As Ray and Boris set their gaff's against the wharf, William loosened the lines that held the *Pacific Lady* at the dock, threw them aboard, and leaped onto the deck, just as the ship had moved eighteen inches away from the pier.

"I'll teach you how to handle the lines when we're at sea," William told Ray. "Captain's a good man. We're like family on this boat. You're replacing my brother Gabriel. Most owners wouldn't have waited to find a temporary replacement for a hurt deckhand, so that the hurt man would have a job when he was well. But Captain McDuff has worked for two weeks with a short crew, doing extra work himself, so that Gabriel would have a job, when his arm is well enough. That says a lot to me," William concluded.

"That's good," Ray agreed, but remained cautious, as he recalled all the suspicion he had faced from the older men at the canning factory.

With the *Pacific Lady* chugging through the bay, William and Boris produced buckets and mops, including one for Ray. "We'll swab the foredeck first, Boris told Ray. "After we're at sea, we'll wash down the holds and pump them out. Then, we'll wash down everything else." Ray loved the feel of the ocean breeze in his face. Once they were out of the sheltered bay and into open water, the *Pacific Lady* began to roll with the big ocean swells. The stench was even worse than it had been at the docks. Most of the ice had melted, so the hold had become hot. Scrubbing the caked blood and fish off the sides of the hold with the big-handled brushes was hard work. Ray became seasick in less than ten minutes, but he never threw up. Once he was back on deck, and some distance from the odor of the rotting fish heat, his seasickness started to recede. Boris took the wheel, while Captain McDuff prepared boiled potatoes, fresh asparagus, and flounder for dinner. "I hope you like fish," the captain laughed. "We eat lots of it out here. It's free."

Ray had eaten fish only rarely, usually when he had gone fishing with his father. Walter loved to catch fresh fish from the South Llano River and fry them in a big iron skillet on a fire he would make by the riverbank. Ray's mother would not allow fish to be cooked in her kitchen, where the odor would linger for days. Captain McDuff's cooking skills fascinated Ray. The flounder was wonderful, and it had been prepared in the closet-like little galley in the boat's cramped cabin. At sea and out of sight of land aboard the *Pacific Lady*, Ray sat down to his first real meal since leaving his parents' home in Telegraph. Mostly in the camps, the men had cooked stew. The other standard fare had been beans and chili, with only beans more often than the more expensive chili meat.

It was almost midnight when the *Pacific Lady* docked in Monterey. Ray had napped for the last two hours of the trip, but was on deck to help moor the ship. Minutes after the *Lady* was secure at the dock, Ray was sleeping soundly on his bunk in the crew's quarters.

"Time to load the ice," Boris told Ray, when he roused him at four a.m. Everyone wore a coat but Ray. The Pacific air was cold and felt much colder because of the eighteen-mile-an-hour breeze blowing down the coast from the Gulf of Alaska. The captain loaned Ray some gloves to work with the ice. Still, Ray was nearly frozen by the time the sun came up. A boy from Texas could never imagine that weather in June could be that cold anywhere, and certainly not in a place the newspapers and radio always called sunny California. Ray loved working on the boat and was actually sad when Gabriel was ready to come back to work. Recalling that his last run-in with California police had come near Monterey, Ray decided to ride the bus back to San Francisco. He wasn't disappointed. The drive was beautiful, and he was having another grand adventure.

CHAPTER EIGHTEEN

Instead of going back to the jungle, Ray found a room for sixty-five cents a night, and began eating most of his meals in diners, while he saw the sights in and around San Francisco. In a week, Ray had three dollars left. He decided to get out of San Francisco, before he had to go back to work in another place like the tuna dock. The night before Ray was to leave San Francisco, he bought a bottle of cheap wine to share with a neighbor at the boarding house where he had rented a room. Ray's new friend spoke with whispered awe about the beauty of Salt Lake City. At length, he described the majesty of the Great Salt Lake, the Temple, and the Wasatch Mountains—filling his description with loving details. Ray never accepted that he was extremely gullible to the suggestions of others. He would hear or read something, and in a matter of minutes, what he had read or heard had become Ray's own original thought. Even through the headache and fog left over by the wine, the next morning, Ray remained convinced that he needed to see Utah. Plotting a course on the map he had borrowed from the school library in Junction, Ray selected the Union Pacific to transport him there.

Interestingly, someone wanting to ride out of California on a freight train went unmolested. Before Ray knew it, he was shivering from the cold again, passing through the Sierra Nevada. The scenery was breathtaking, but Ray reminded himself that he had to bring a coat on his next trip—no matter what the weather was in Texas. The fast freight was rolling for Chicago like a passenger train. There had been no boxcars on the train, only reefers filled with fruit and vegetables, plus half a dozen empty gondola cars. Ray was riding in the lead gondola pushed up against the end nearest the adjacent icebox car. He had been hoping to find some shelter from the skin numbing wind. As soon as the train moved into the Nevada desert, Ray was fully exposed to a blistering sun. The wind generated by the train's speed kept the ride from being too hot, but the sun was merciless. Keeping to his rule not to sleep on a train as it headed into a city, Ray jumped off the gondola car and spent the night under a highway bridge in Elko, Nevada. No one bothered him. And the next morning, Ray was riding in another gondola car headed east once more on an equally fast train. The temperature on the Bonneville Salt Flats approaching the lake was easily over a hundred degrees, and Ray was quickly drying out in the sun. He concluded that he should have bought a canteen in California, when he still had some money. The big Salt Lake's call to Ray pulled him off the train like a magnet. He detrained as the freight waited on a siding near the lake for a westbound train to pass. One of the stories Ray's neighbor in the rooming house had told him was about how easily people floated in the heavy salt water of the gigantic lake. Ray was fascinated by the idea. Besides, the whole time he had been in California, he had been dying to swim in the Pacific but had never gotten the chance. In Santa Monica, he had not been able to swim because he did not have a suit. Captain McDuff had refused to let him swim off his boat because the water in the open ocean was too cold.

Ray almost ran the mile from the tracks to the lake. No one was around, so he stripped off his clothes and dashed into the water. He floated in the heavy lake water for nearly an hour, exhilarated by the experience. When he came out of the water, Ray was weak from thirst. His face and chest were extremely sunburned, and tiny blisters covered his body. There was no shelter from the sun, either by the lake or at the tracks. Seven eastbound trains passed without pulling into the siding. When at last an eastbound train stopped, Ray had become delirious from his exposure to the sun and dehydration. Using the last of his strength Ray managed to crawl into a gondola car still coated with rust from an earlier load of scrap metal. An hour later, when the train pulled into the yard in Salt Lake City, Ray's appearance was frightening. He had fever, the blisters from his sunburn had begun to burst, and his skin and clothes were covered with rust and dirt. It was nearly ten o'clock at night. Ray found a rooming house not far from the yards run by a starched and well-washed Mormon woman. She took Ray's money, told him where the bath was, and where to sleep. Despite his condition, Ray managed a bath, then fell deeply asleep. At breakfast the next morning, the table was spread with fresh bread, hot cereals, milk, ham, and scrambled eggs. Ray tried to drink some coffee, but it was too hot for his parched tongue. He downed several glasses of water before the sister of the lady who had taken his money told Ray two men were waiting to see him. Dazed by the fever, Ray blindly followed as the woman led him through the kitchen to the back door.

"They're waiting outside," the woman told him. As Ray walked onto the first back step, two hands he did not see grabbed his left arm and jerked him into the back yard. As he fell, a nightstick crashed into the back of Ray's neck. "Who told you bums were welcome in Salt Lake City?" one of the police officers growled. Ray never heard the snarled condemnation. He had been knocked out by the first blow from the cop's club. But unconsciousness didn't save Ray from a savage beating at the hands of the two self-righteous lawmen. When they were finished, the policemen dragged Ray to their patrol car, lifted him into the back seat, and drove him to a freight yard. The officers found a railroad security guard, who had a master padlock key. The Union Pacific detective opened a car that was chilled by dry ice to a temperature that was maintained at forty-two degrees. The three men threw Ray inside and locked the door. Most, but not all the cars were scheduled to go to Chicago. A grocer in Omaha found Ray, when he opened the door to the car the next morning, as he and two of his employees were unloading a shipment of lettuce from Salinas. Ray had a slight pulse when the ambulance attendants removed him from the reefer, but it would be ten days before he woke from his coma in a hospital. Even then, the pneumonia was so severe that doctors were convinced

Ray would die. Walter boarded a train in Junction with a heavy heart, believing his son would be dead by the time he got to Omaha.

Ray lived, but Walter had to wait two weeks in Omaha before his son was well enough to travel home. Ray had lost forty pounds during his ordeal. Ada had been so devastated, and so deeply hurt by Ray's thoughtless behavior that she had to force herself to begin the process of nursing Ray back to health. Ultimately, she could not give up on the frail child she had brought back from death so many times before. She couldn't stop loving her children, no matter how foolish or hurtful their behavior and misdeeds were, no matter how much their actions had hurt her.

CHAPTER NINETEEN

During his senior year, Ray was out of Brooks' shadow for the first time in his life. Being one of the few players with real ability, Ray buckled down and became a football hero in his own right. For the most part, Junction was an average football team without Brooks, helping Ray become a standout—perhaps good enough for a scholarship at Southwest Texas State Teachers College in San Marcos or one of the state's lesser-known colleges with a football program. As Ray had tagged along with Brooks for his first day of school—in much the same fashion, when Brooks was finished with school, so was Ray. He was bored. Ignoring the possibility of playing at a higher level, when the football season ended at Junction High School, Ray was back riding freight trains. He took three trips during his final year in school and came home twice with pneumonia, and once with gonorrhea, a disease he did not reveal to his mother. Despite these lengthy absences, Ray graduated near the top of his class.

For the summer after graduation, Walter managed to keep Ray off freight trains by getting him a job with the Southern Pacific unloading general freight in San Antonio. The hard physical work suited Ray well, and the money it paid kept him in whiskey and drinking companions. Ray came face to face with disappointment when he talked with his parents in late August.

"Ray, you have a fine mind. But so far in your life, you have wasted everything God has given you," Ada had begun. After pausing for a minute, she handed her youngest son an envelope. "There's five-hundred dollars in here. It's what I got when Mother sold the farm on the Pedernales and moved to Oklahoma. There's also a train ticket your father arranged for you. I want you to take this money, and get on up to Texas A&M. It's time you stopped wasting your life, and make something of yourself," Ada said sternly to her youngest son. Tears trickled down Ray's cheeks. "Momma, I can't take your money," he said before dropping the envelope back in Ada's open purse. Ada began to sob deeply. And in a second, she had bolted from the parlor of the boarding house in San Antonio, where Ray lived, and taken refuge on the porch. Ray and Walter stood alone in the big room, where Ada's crying penetrated, not only their ears, but their souls, as well.

"Ray, I've watched for years as you've broken your mother's heart. Don't you care about anybody but yourself, ever?" Walter asked.

"Papa, I don't want to hurt her, but I can't take her money and go to College Station. I'd hate it there, and I'd be gone in a few days, and so would much of her money. She would be even more hurt then," Ray explained.

"Well what are you going to do with your life, son? Are you going to just ride around on freight trains until someone kills you?"

"Why can't I just stay here?" Ray appealed to his father. "I like it here. I'm making good money and ... "

Walter interrupted. "How much money do you have right now?"

"None," Ray answered. "But I'll get paid on Saturday."

Walter resumed, "And you'll drink that all up, just like you have all the rest of the money you've made this summer?"

Ray shrugged. "It's what I like to do." The expression on Walter's face was calm but conveyed his wisdom. "It'll kill you, son—and sooner than you have any idea. Your mother's crying her heart out. Let's see if we can come up with *something*," his father urged.

Ray gave honest thought to what his father had just requested. "Edythe lives in Tyler," Ray suggested. "There's a junior college up there. She's written me twice this summer trying to get me to go to school there and live with her. If I tried that, would that make you and Momma happy?"

"It's worth a try," Walter agreed immediately. Ada went along with Ray's proposal, but she just couldn't wait for a train. She'd had all of this place she could stand. Walter borrowed a car from the district manager of the Southern Pacific, and the Oakleys spent the next two days driving Ray to Tyler. "I hope he stays and goes to school," Ada confided to her husband as they began the long, bumpy trip back to San Antonio in the district manager's car. In truth, neither parent believed there was much chance that Ray would stick with the college for long. Even on such a long trip as they faced between Tyler and Junction, Ada and Walter couldn't bring themselves to talk aloud about Ray's problems anymore. Both their minds were filled with concerns. Both spent a lot of effort trying to figure out what made Ray act the way he did. Sometimes, Walter would talk with his friends at the courthouse about his son. On the other hand, Ada never said anything about Ray to anyone outside the family.

The behavior of their children was a persistent puzzle troubling Ada and Walter. As much as they searched their own past, and that of their parents, aunts, and uncles, they could find few clues as to why so many bad things seemed to happen to their children. Neither parent was willing to think of any of the children, not even Glenn, as evil. They were all extremely headstrong. All were rebellious and determined to make their own way; and all, except for Ray, and the almost never mentioned Glenn, were extremely ambitious.

Ada and Walter could hardly think of Glenn at all. To the extent they admitted to themselves that their son had done bad things, they blamed those acts on alcohol and drugs. In fact, excluding his drinking binges, which usually led Glenn to run away from home, Glenn had seldom shown meanness as a child. Glenn had lived, and died without Ada and Walter ever learning how Ralph's bullying had tormented their second son. They never knew how hurt Glenn had been during his years at home. Glenn never let anyone, except for Ralph and Jimmy Barnes know how deeply Ralph's hate had cut into him. One thing everyone in the family knew about Glenn was that he was not like any of the rest of them. His stature was much smaller, and he was not nearly as bright as the rest of the Oakleys. Toward the end of his life, he expressed a determination to get even, which was manifested by his use of guns. Even then, Glenn did not strike directly at Ralph, the person who had made him suffer most.

Indeed, when Glenn's anguish so overwhelmed him that he tried to destroy his only friend bit by bit, Glenn did not shoot Ralph. Neither did Glenn shoot himself. He tormented and hurt his friend so completely that Jimmy Barnes was all but forced to fire the shot that killed Glenn. Had Glenn's extreme mistreatment of his best friend Jimmy been Glenn's tortured means of suicide? No one could or would ever know. Never aloud, but often in the silence of their separate minds, when both parents were in deep pain from worrying about the tragic condition of one or more of their children, Ada and Walter would wonder where the collection of bad forces that had ruined Glenn's life had come from. It was the deepest mystery in the Oakley family.

Ralph was also mystifying. He seemed on the surface to have the best of both his parents. He was the boy who had the world at his feet. Yes, Ralph had tormented Glenn harshly, and he had tried to punish Brooks and Ray as well. When you got right down to things, Ralph had no sense of direction. His only obvious motivating force was greed. Maryon, Jimmie, Edythe, Brooks, and Ruth all wanted to excel. They strove to capture as much of the world as their capabilities would permit. Ralph seemed only to want to accumulate money. He wanted to keep everyone around him, especially his brothers and sisters, from having anything of importance that he did not control. Ralph's greed was a sickness that hurt him, and everyone in his life. He could not understand why his father was so weak, why his father would not control and dominate others. Ralph seemed determined to make up for what he viewed as Walter's lack of assertiveness. Ray, in many ways, was as selfish as Ralph. Ray was not greedy for money. Ray's greed was for freedom to act on whatever whim that seized him at any given moment. He did not want his mother to cry when he rode off on a freight train, but Ray never suffered enough guilt to stop him from doing whatever outlandish thing he developed an urge to do. Like

Ralph, Ray hated what he, too, believed was Walter's weakness. Even when confronted with the power Walter could exercise in far reaching parts of Texas, even when told by people as unattached to Junction as the Farmer, what his father had achieved in helping to build the Southern Pacific, Ray continued to see a weak man every time he looked at his father.

Ray was also like Glenn in one way. Inside, he was alone. One important force kept Ray from suffering the way Glenn and Ralph had. It was Ray's older brother, Brooks. From the beginning of his life, Brooks set Ray in a positive direction and put him back on the right track repeatedly. These two brothers were held together almost by a magnetic field or gravitational pull. As far as he ran from Junction, Ray never freed himself of Brooks' influence. Brooks also exerted a significant influence on other members of the family, even on his parents. But none of the others needed Brooks' guidance as much as Ray. Moreover, no one loved Brooks as much as Ray did. Ray's love for Brooks came close to being a genuine worship. Ralph's resentment of Brooks' influence never abated. Ralph could not hope to dominate the family, could never attain the status he was due as eldest son, because his little brother had this captivating influence over the entire Oakley family. Ralph never stopped hating Brooks, and he would never quit trying to destroy Brooks.

CHAPTER TWENTY

From the moment they began living together, things between Ray and Edythe were severely strained. To Edythe, her physically large little brother seemed pushy. Concerned that Ray would run off, she tried hard not to alienate him, which became more difficult after Ray's first day at Tyler Junior College. He hated it immediately, and he went to class for only two weeks before catching a freight train east. When Edythe did not answer her mother's letters asking about how Ray was doing in school, Ada knew that Ray had disappeared. About two weeks after he left Tyler, Ray showed up at Maryon's house in Pittsburgh. She had moved to Pennsylvania with her new husband after a dreadfully painful recovery from her first marriage. On most of his train ride to Pittsburgh, Ray had been locked in another refrigerator car without a coat. He had a bad cold when he reached his sister's house, but he was not seriously ill. Maryon's husband bought Ray a ticket back to Tyler; but before he had a chance to give it to Ray, the wayward brother was on another freight train, heading home to Texas. Ray sent his mother a telegram telling her he was back with Edythe, in good health, and ready to enroll in school again.

Tyler Junior College was not as enthused about Ray's plan as their wayward student was. The college told Ray that he would have to sit out the spring term. That came as part of the academic probation the school had placed Ray on. Ada might be almost four hundred miles away, but her daughter Edythe could feel her mother's wishes—so much so that Ada might just as well be sitting across the room from her daughter. Edythe came up with a new plan. There was also a private commercial business college in Tyler. Even though classes had been in progress for a week, and despite Ray's poor attendance at Tyler Junior College, Edythe was able to convince the school to accept her brother. Eleven weeks later, Ray graduated at the top of his class at Tyler Commercial College, complete with a certificate proclaiming that Amos Ray Oakley was a bookkeeper.

Like most Texas towns, Tyler was at the mercy of the booms and busts of the oil business. For the moment, jobs were scarce in Tyler. However, Ray had another big sister living nearby. In a few days, Jimmie had found Ray a job keeping books for a local independent oil company in Gladewater, and Ray moved from one sister's house to another. In addition to keeping track of the company's money, Ray sometimes drove the big trucks hauling crude out of the oil fields to the cracking plant a few miles away. There, the crude would be broken down into separate components before being shipped to one of the giant refineries in Port Arthur, Nederland, or Beaumont. On days when a crew was short, Ray worked as a roughneck twelve or fourteen hours each day. At night, he drank, played pool, and brawled with the oil field workers in the nearby beer joints. Ray regularly came to work with a black eye or sutures. One injury required his jaws to be wired shut for six weeks. Ray was having the time of his life.

Jimmie and Edythe kept Ada supplied with letters about Ray's well-being, leaving out the parts about drinking, fighting, and frequent overnight stays in various jails. Because Ray had a steady, well-paying job, local police chiefs and sheriffs would always have him out in time for work, no matter what time he had been locked up the night, or early morning, before. Ray always stood good for his bail or fine. And charges that could easily have been categorized as felonies for less responsible offenders were reduced to misdemeanors and sometimes dismissed outright. At any rate, it was not like Ray Oakley was the only barroom brawler in the oil patch. It was an unruly time and place. The fact that Ray was staying put gave his mother at least some comfort.

There were other major life changing events happening in the Oakley family. Ray's older brother Brooks had established a life for himself in Austin running the city's only all-night restaurant, the Longhorn Waffle Shop, an Austin institution on Congress Avenue just a few blocks south of the State Capitol. Brooks had also shocked everyone who knew him when he joined the Texas National Guard.

When he reported to Fort Sam Houston in San Antonio for basic training, the drill sergeant told Brooks "You should be an officer, son," after he discovered that Brooks was only two courses short of receiving a Bachelor of Science degree from U.T.

"No thank you," Brooks told the sergeant. As he worked through his training, Brooks also had to convince several officers that he did not want a commission. But his protests did not end the badgering. Ray stayed in Gladewater far longer than anyone could have predicted, but left after a falling out with his boss, the owner of the company. Ray bummed around on freight trains for a while before settling in Corpus Christi. The Great Depression refused to release its chokehold on America's economy. In 1937, the country was knocked to its economic knees a second time. Ray couldn't find work as a bookkeeper, so he took a job on a construction crew building a pipeline. He said he liked working outdoors better, even when he spent his whole day in a ditch in hundred-degree weather. Ray learned life's conventions the hard way, when he learned them at all.

In Junction, the post of county judge came open. Sheriff Wilson and the county commissioners drove to the Oakley farm. Each of the four commissioners, speaking one at a time, asked Walter to accept an emergency appointment as judge, and promised their cooperation on the court. Walter was told that no one would run against him if he would accept the job and agree to run for a full term in the next election. Sheriff Wilson was the last to contribute. "Ada," he said, speaking directly to his old friend. "Without even asking, I know you're against this. I suspect that if you decide to, you can stop Walter from taking up this responsibility. But I want to ask you as a personal favor not to do that. Kimble County has had outstanding leadership. And now, with our native son Coke serving as governor, we need Walter in charge of our county government, so we don't slip back to where we were before. I know as well as you that Walter has given enough. And I know with your kids all out of the house now, you'd like to have some time with him. But the fact is, Ada, Walter likes doing what he does. He can't just sit out here on this farm. This is really Miguel's business, here. We need Walter's help in town. He's the only man in the county who can get along with everybody. He's the only person we know of who can keep different parts of the county from fighting among themselves. And the fact is, Ada, that Walter will enjoy this job, if you'll let him. I'm sorry I had to say things this way, but we've been friends for a long time, and I just had to tell you what I thought."

"It's all right, Bill," Ada responded softly. "It's not what I would choose, but I know you're right. I won't stand in the way if being county judge is what Walter wants." Tension whooshed out of the room when Ada finished her answer.

Walter stood up. "Well gentlemen, I am very flattered with what you said about me. I don't think I agree with very much of it, but I am honored that you have asked me," Walter announced with a smile that brought a collective nervous laughter from everyone. "I hope you'll give Ada and me some time to think this over and talk about it. If she'll go," Walter said looking over at his wife, "I think I'll take her into San Antone. We used to do that every year, but we haven't been able to go for a long time now. Anyway, I'd like to have a couple of days to mull things over if you can wait that long." The commissioners agreed, speaking in near unison. "Take whatever time you need, and let us know when you get back," Sheriff Wilson said as he rose to end the meeting.

For Ada and Walter, the trip to San Antonio became a time to remember. They stayed in a hotel, ate in restaurants, and walked along the river. Ada went shopping at Joske's. Walter visited old friends at the railroad office; but mostly, Ada and Walter had time to sit and talk. "Bill Wilson's right," Ada told her husband. "Just like Papa said, Walter

—you'll never make a farmer. You'd much rather be down at the courthouse than sitting home getting old. You know how I hate politics, but my hating something won't change it. You take the job, Walter. That's what you should do," Ada finished, emphasizing the word "should." A few days later, Walter took the oath and became Kimble County Judge.

CHAPTER TWENTY-ONE

Brooks' enlistment in the National Guard was scheduled to end just as Hitler began rearranging Europe. The talk of war in Texas was faint, but Brooks heard it and felt that U.S. involvement was inevitable. He often expressed his dislike of the military and told more than one listener at the coffee counter in the Longhorn how disappointed his father had been when Brooks had refused to consider an appointment to West Point. But in what would seem to be a contradiction of his disdain for all things related to the military, Brooks signed up for another four years in the Guard, and once again rejected a renewed offer to become an officer. He was a sergeant with three stripes the day Pearl Harbor was bombed, and his orders arrived the following Friday. Sunday night, December 14, 1941, Brooks reported to Fort Sam Houston. He was surprised to be there because he had spent most of his time at Camp Mabry in Austin, the Guard's headquarters. The regular Army was already well represented at Fort Sam, which was soon to be overflowing with new volunteers who had enlisted to become soldiers. Fort Sam Houston was also the home of one of the Army's rising stars, General Dwight Eisenhower, who had been immediately summoned to Washington by Army Chief of Staff General George Marshall just hours after the Japanese attacked Hawaii.

During the drive to San Antonio, Brooks had wondered what the significance of his being assigned to Fort Sam might be. The National Guard was controlled by Texas politicians through Camp Mabry. Brooks chose to re-enlist, figuring it would keep him in Austin and prevent him from being shipped overseas. Now, with the war less than a week old, he was already out of Austin. Did that mean he was on his way overseas? As he pulled up to the gate of the fort, Brooks had begun to consider that he might have outsmarted himself. The next morning, he was at work before noon. He had been made company clerk for a regular Army unit that needed someone with his skills as a bookkeeper, typist, and expert in Army travel regulations. When he spoke to the captain, he learned that it was uncertain whether his assignment was temporary. He was told to keep his Texas guard patches on his uniform for the time being.

"Level with me, captain. What are our chances of going overseas?" Brooks asked that first morning.

"Why, sergeant?" the captain responded with a challenge? "Are you afraid to fight?"

Maintaining his composure and attempting to add extra calm to his expressions and tone, Brooks replied, "No sir. I have a business to run in Austin. I expected to be called up if war broke out, but I thought it would be at Camp Mabry. If we're shipping out, I have a lot of arrangements to make."

The captain relaxed, perhaps assured that the National Guard had not saddled him with a coward. He looked down at the paper on his desk.

"Oakley, I wish I could help you," he said. "This is a military police company. Nothing in the Army moves without M.P.'s, so we could be on our way to England, or Hawaii, or the Philippines before you can bat an eye. They might also send us to a place like Fort Dix in New Jersey or San Francisco, where they'll be loading out for both theaters, Atlantic and Pacific. I doubt anyone knows yet. As I said earlier, I don't know whether we'll even keep you. You might be headed back to a guard unit. But you might want to start your arrangements just in case you are shipped out with us."

Brooks was now certain that he had gotten himself into a fine mess. By afternoon, he was typing travel orders and vouchers for soldiers and guardsmen from all over the country, bringing them to San Antonio. That's all he did for two weeks, write papers bringing massive numbers of soldiers to Fort Sam. Usually, he didn't finish his work until eleven o'clock at night. As soon as he finished each evening, Brooks was on the phone to the Longhorn, preparing for the restaurant to operate without him during what Brooks was certain would be an extended period. Brooks wrote Walter a detailed letter, asking him to do several things aimed at making sure Brooks' personal business would be in order in the event Brooks was sent overseas. Brooks was totally convinced that he would never come home if he got into actual combat. He didn't tell anyone, but in his mind, Brooks was certain this is the way things would go. For several days, Brooks internally debated the notion of going on sick call. His ankle was hurting from all the long hours. It hurt no worse than it had in the restaurant. But the pain was very real, as was the condition that caused it. Surely, if the doctor were any good at all, Brooks was unlikely to be certified as fit for combat. He kept his X-rays in the top drawer of his desk just in case.

Finally, Brooks rejected the idea of going on sick call. He was not a coward, and he did not want anyone to think of him as one. If Brooks had wanted to use his injury to avoid combat, he should have taken the X-rays with him to the physical examination conducted when he joined the guard. In Brooks' mind, using those pictures to get out of going to war six years later would mark him a coward forever. At Fort Sam Houston, Brooks was buried in travel orders and vouchers for railroad tickets. Most of the rest of the units floundered. But in Brooks' company, new people were moved in efficiently, and the people who were being assigned to other units left when they were supposed to. So when someone messed up the travel orders of Colonel Nathan Scholz, the irate officer was passed along to Brooks. As he entered, he saw five Texas National Guardsmen furiously typing. The room was clouded with cigarette smoke, and Brooks sat barely visible near an open window across the room from the door. The top of Brooks' bald head could just barely be seen behind the huge stack of folders on his desk. Scholz tapped the desk of the private closest to the door.

"On your feet, soldier," he barked. The young man looked up pleasantly but kept the typewriter moving smoothly across the page.

"Can I help you, sir?" the guardsman inquired.

"Don't they even teach you people in the National Guard how to salute an officer?" Scholz demanded.

"Yes sir," the private responded, continuing to smile. "But General Fitzsimmons said that since this seems to be the only outfit in the Army that knows how to put a soldier on a train, that we ought to do what we're doing and let him worry about the officers. Can we help you, sir?"

Scholz was seething, but he was already two days late getting back to Washington. He decided not to pursue the matter with this grinning idiot whose fingers seemed to be glued to his typewriter keys. "Where's Sergeant Oakley?" the obnoxious lieutenant colonel demanded.

"He's back there," the guardsman said, removing one hand from his keyboard just long enough to point a finger toward Brooks' desk.

"Well junior, you get your behind back there and tell him Colonel Nathan Scholz is here to see him," Scholz growled, his face now glowing red from anger. While the young recruit gasped for air, Brooks stepped quickly to his rescue. He popped a smart salute to the colonel, which the colonel returned out of shock. Brooks spoke efficiently and politely before the colonel could resume the tirade he had been directing at the private.

"Colonel, if you'll sign here and here, and initial in these four places I have marked, you'll be on your way to Washington. There's a jeep waiting outside for you, sir," Brooks said, making certain he had an appropriately respectful smile for the pompous bag of wind standing in front of him.

"Well that's more like it," Scholz said beaming. He grabbed the pen from Brooks' hand and scrawled some letters where Brooks was pointing. Brooks accepted the pen back in one hand, snapped a second salute with his other, and moved quickly to open the door. "Your jeep is right over there, sir," Brooks said, gesturing toward a vehicle fifty feet away that sat with the motor running and a driver standing beside it. Scholz was out the door, proud of himself for having shocked some military discipline into those greenhorn guardsmen. Finally after days of inertia, he was on his way back to Washington. He sat with one foot propped on the edge of the cutout left in the body of the open jeep. The cutout was part of the jeep's design. It had been left so the vehicle could be closed in by snapping on a cloth door and top. Scholz was so pleased with himself that he was whistling as the driver dodged his way through the crunch of civilian cars, military trucks, and jeeps that seemed to be everywhere in San Antonio. In less than ten minutes, the corporal driving the jeep screeched to a halt and jumped out grabbing for the colonel's luggage.

"Here we are, sir," he chirped. The blood vessels close to the surface of the lieutenant colonel's face had exploded, turning his entire face a fiery red again. The jeep was parked in front of a train station.

"You idiot," Scholz bellowed, "we're supposed to be at the airport."

The terrified jeep driver fumbled with an attempted apology. "I'm sorry sir. The sergeant told me to bring you to the depot, and I just thought he knew what he was talking about."

Scholz ripped the papers out of his jacket pocket. His orders said travel by train, and the voucher Brooks had given him was for a railroad ticket. He burst into the station, and across the lobby to a pay phone. In a second, he screamed into the phone.

"This is Colonel Scholz for General Fitzsimmons." The young lady on the phone jumped up from her desk when the man's screaming invaded her ear, then took a deep breath before she spoke. "Hold on please, colonel," she said, then pushed down the hold button on her phone.

"Captain, this is that awful lieutenant colonel from Washington, and he sounds hopping mad," she called to the officer through the open door a few feet from her desk.

"I'll talk to him," the captain said, smiling, then pausing for a deep breath before picking up the phone. "Colonel, this is Captain Biggs. The general is in a meeting right now. Can I help you with something?" he asked politely.

"It's that impudent Sergeant Oakley," Scholz said, steaming at having to talk to an aide instead of the general. "He's put me on a train for Washington, and I need to get there tonight."

Captain Biggs was apologetic. "I am sorry, sir. Maybe there was a mistake. If you want, I'll ... "

Scholz cut him off. "Oh, there was no mistake. Oakley thought it would be cute to insult some visiting brass from out of town. But if he thinks he can get away with that with me, that little smart aleck's got another think coming. When can I talk to your boss?" Scholz huffed.

"It may be some time, colonel. He's got a major staff meeting going," Biggs explained.

"And you're not in there, captain?" Scholz snapped.

"Well sir, it looked like it was going to last most of the afternoon, so I ducked out to catch up on some paperwork. If there's some way he can reach you, I'll have the general call you as soon as he's through with the meeting. The very first thing," Biggs offered calmly.

"I'm at a payphone, captain," Scholz spat through the phone. Captain Biggs was ready to try another approach, but Scholz hung up.

Two weeks later, Scholz' boss, General Hershey, was on a visit to Fort Sam Houston. The minute he finished his meeting with General Fitzsimmons, the two generals went directly to Brooks' work area. As the two generals burst through the door, Brooks' staff of guardsmen shot to their feet and saluted. Before he returned the salutes, General Hershey turned to General Fitzsimmons. "So these guardsmen do know how to salute, general," he said, keeping a stern face. Only Brooks was not terrified. He knew that two generals had not come to chew him out. They told colonels to tell captains to do things like that. This was something more sinister than a dressing down about military discipline. Brooks braced himself as he moved toward the two generals.

"Brooks," General Fitzsimmons spoke, as Brooks approached. "This is General Lewis Hershey. He wanted to meet you." Turning to General Hershey, General Fitzsimmons said, "General, this is Sergeant Brooks Oakley." General Hershey extended his hand, and Brooks shook it, watching the general's eyes carefully, looking for a clue that would reveal to Brooks what this business was about.

"Son," the general blurted, "I wanted to meet the sergeant who could send my aide back to Washington on a train." The room fell silent. Brooks realized he was the one who was supposed to speak next.

"I was just following the general's own orders, sir," Brooks responded cautiously after a pause that he felt seemed far too long to comply with the standards of correct military protocol.

"Well, it's nice to know someone in this Army reads the orders I send out. Here," the general continued, handing a large brown envelope over to Brooks. "These orders will send you to Officer's Candidate School at Fort Benning on tomorrow morning's train," General Hershey continued as Brooks kept his eyes studiously locked on the suspicious general's eyes. Brooks was dumbstruck. He zipped through his mind, searching for the words that would stop the steamroller he could already feel was about to crush him.

"I understand that you read regulations as thoroughly as you read orders," the general said sternly. "So you either know, or will soon know, that you have the right to refuse these orders. To save us a lot of trouble, sergeant," the general said, producing a second envelope that General Fitzsimmons had been holding underneath his arm, "I've drawn up an alternate set of orders that the manual won't permit you to refuse. These second orders say that, if you elect not to go to Fort Benning, your pigheaded butt will be on the first ship to the Pacific Theatre." The room was so quiet that the ordinary sounds of men breathing echoed like thunder.

"Nice to meet you, son. You'll make a fine officer," the general said, shaking Brooks' hand again. The two generals were gone in seconds. The next morning, Brooks was on the train to Fort Benning. Ninety hellish days later, he was riding another train to Washington with the shiny gold bars of a newly commissioned second lieutenant resting nervously on his shoulders.

Part Two
FALLEN SISTERS

CHAPTER TWENTY-TWO

"It's just not fair!" Maryon proclaimed angrily. "My average is three points higher than Horace Mueller's. If I can't be valedictorian, I just won't go to graduation. I earned this honor, Mother. Horace Mueller didn't." Maryon, Ada and Walter's oldest daughter, was the best at everything. She was captain of the basketball team, star of the senior play, and her picture appeared in her high school yearbook above the caption "Most Beautiful." Being beautiful was easier for Maryon than for most young ladies. She took it as a great honor and kept it as a privilege to be maintained. Maryon's gift of beauty was even more special to her, because it was such a delight to her father. Walter's expressions of joy and pride were predictable, automatic and punctuated with a special laugh.

At home on their farm along the South Llano River, Maryon was Ada's best friend. Sometimes that was difficult for Maryon. She enjoyed their friendship, but with so many younger brothers and sisters, Maryon had been a little girl for only a short time. Too many children needed her attention. The difficult talk mother and daughter were having about Maryon not being allowed to take her rightful place as class valedictorian was not only heartbreaking, but it was fraught with any number of potential pitfalls. Mistakes and careless words spoken about this issue had the potential to last a lifetime.

"You are absolutely right," Ada agreed. Maryon had more than enough reasons to raise the roof about the grievous wrong that was being done to her. "You did earn this honor, and the school is wrong to steal it from you. Like many things in life, this is completely wrong and grossly unfair, but Junction is a small town, and no girl has ever been valedictorian here before."

Maryon was furious, because something very special was being snatched away from her. But helping Ada with the children had taught her to sacrifice. "If I don't go to graduation, you and Dad will be very disappointed, won't you?" Maryon asked. "We are already livid, because you have been hurt so deeply and so unfairly, maliciously actually. And I have never seen your father so upset with people who should know better," Ada responded.

"Oh, it's not our friends and neighbors, and it's certainly not the teachers. Some of them have even offered to quit if I don't get to be valedictorian. The problem is coming from a few old fuddy-duddies who think women should only have babies, not brains," Maryon stormed. Ada was shocked by the crude way her daughter expressed herself, but she knew Maryon was right. The room was quiet for a few minutes. When Maryon spoke again, she was calm. "Mrs. Shepherd has an idea," Maryon offered. "And I think I will do what she suggested.," Maryon said. "Your father and I will support whatever you decide to do," Ada responded. "We love you very much."

At the graduation ceremony, Maryon's chair on stage next to Horace Mueller sat empty. One of the teachers attempted to remove it, but the principal insisted it be left as it was. Maryon did not speak as salutatorian, when her name was called. After a long silence, a few people stood and applauded in salute to Maryon's unspoken protest. Quickly, most of the audience rose, vigorously clapping their hands in support of Junction High's most accomplished graduate. Maryon appeared on stage twice: to receive her diploma, and when her scholarship to Baylor University was presented. She cried only once, when she saw her mother and father standing and clapping the last time she walked off the stage.

Maryon loved her parents absolutely, but she could not wait until fall to get away from Junction. The morning after graduation, she was on a train heading to New Mexico. She delighted in a magical summer riding her new horse on her grandparents' farm and relished in a wonderful excursion to Santa Fe with her amazing grandmother Rebecca.

At home in Telegraph, Ada prayed that Jimmie would find a better path for her life after Maryon went away to college. Jimmie's mother agonized, hoping that not having to compete face to face with her exceptional sister would smooth Jimmie's troubled journey toward adulthood. Even though Walter had grown up in a big family, he seemed to understand nothing about children. Ada blamed that on the circumstances of Walter's early life along New Mexico's Little Hatchet Creek, where he had never had a chance to be a child. Walter had begun doing grownup work beside his father, when he was five. Still Ada was often frustrated at her husband's seeming lack of recognition and inability to express empathy no matter how many attempts Ada had made to explain her fears to Walter.

"Jimmie could never hope to compete with someone as beautiful and talented as Maryon. Walter, I can't believe you don't see that," Ada often scolded. "Now that Maryon and Ralph are away from home, I hope Jimmie'll bloom and quit being such a tomboy." Ada never mentioned the name of her son Glenn, who had experienced such a tragic life and death.

"Now mother," Walter said, hoping to soothe Ada a bit. "Jimmie is every bit as pretty as her sister. Everybody says she has the most beautiful red hair they have ever seen."

"Walter, you're impossible," an exasperated Ada replied. "Don't patronize me. Jimmie's sixteen years old, and she still fights with the boys, and plays football with them, too. Why, Mrs. Simmons said that last spring Jimmie was out behind the gym smoking with the boys before school let out for the day."

Hoping to calm his wife, Walter would offer his explanation. "Maryon did the same things.

"She did not, Walter Oakley!" Ada fumed. Ada had a blind spot where Maryon was concerned. She had never been able to see anything about her oldest daughter, except intelligence, beauty, poise and maturity. Walter knew there was no use correcting Ada. She would only get angrier, but sometimes he could not contain his own mischief. "I suppose so," he said, his smile broadening. "But Maryon did whip Jimmy Birdwell the summer she was fifteen—and he was the captain of the football team."

"She did not," Ada protested. "Besides, he was being mean to her horse." They enjoyed a laugh together. Ada would not admit she was wrong, but she did pull her husband's ear playfully before scolding him again. "Now get out of my kitchen," she said, unable to contain her smile. "I've got work to do."

Maryon went to Baylor, and Jimmie became the sweetheart of Junction High School. Her mother was right. Jimmie could not compete with her sister, even if Maryon was two-hundred miles away. She had none of Maryon's poise and confidence. Jimmie covered her insecurity with a gruff and often crude exterior. She smoked with the boys, cussed with the boys, and by spring, she was drinking with the boys, too. Away from home, Maryon was caught up in the new era sweeping the country. They called it the Jazz Age in the New York papers, magazines, and books. In Baptist Waco, this new, anything goes behavior, was strongly condemned as sinful, a one-way trip to hell. After a few weeks in school, Maryon began to find Waco as confining as Junction had been. "I can't wait for summer, so I can come back to your farm and ride horses," Maryon wrote to her grandparents.

But her thoughts of New Mexico were transitory. She rode a small train called the Interurban to Dallas with her new friend Beasley. They were going to spend the weekend with Beasley's parents who, as it turned out, were actually in New York on a business trip. Maryon's letter to her sister was a celebration of her newfound freedom.

My Darling Sister,

I had the most wonderful time of my life in Dallas this weekend. Beasley and I went shopping at the most fabulous store in the world called Neiman Marcus. We bought dresses just like the ones they have pictures of in Vogue magazine. Of course I didn't have enough money to pay for my dress, but they let me charge it to Daddy. I don't know what I'm going to do when he gets the bill, but I'll worry about that later.

We spent the whole day shopping and that night we went to a place called the country club for dinner. I got to drink champagne, and I felt just like a movie star sitting with all those beautiful people. We danced until eleven o'clock. After the dancing, Beasley's aunt told us we might go for a ride in Murphy Webster's car. He has a brand-new Stutz Bearcat, and we drove all over Dallas with the top down.

He is the most handsome man I have ever seen. He was dressed in a tuxedo. He held doors open for me, and he let me smoke cigarettes in public right in his car as we drove down Main Street. He is just home from Yale and helping in his father's bank until he decides what he wants to do in New York. I hope he likes me. I must run. It's very late.

Your loving sister,
Maryon

"Get out of here!" Jimmie screamed at Edythe and slammed the door.

"Jimmie, what's the matter?" Ada asked sternly.

"That little brat is always spying on me," Jimmie answered crossly.

"I was just trying to read her letter," Edythe explained, blinking her innocent young eyes at her mother.

"You got your own letter from Maryon dear. We all did," Ada said, hoping to placate the feuding sisters.

"But mine is not juicy like Jimmie's," Edythe pouted.

"Mother!" Jimmie screamed.

"Come on dear. I need some help in the kitchen, and your sister has homework to do," Ada instructed Edythe, as she began directing her away from Jimmie's rage.

CHAPTER TWENTY-THREE

Jimmie was furious. Maryon already had her hooks into the most beautiful man in Texas, and Jimmie was stuck with a bunch of farmers in the Hill Country. She fumed for weeks, as more letters came telling Jimmie what a wonderful dancer Murphy was, what amazing new place he had taken her to, and how rich he was. "Of course he can't wait to marry me," Maryon wrote. "But mother would kill me!"

Walter and Ada got fewer letters, and none of them mentioned Murphy. Maryon did warn her father about the bill for the dress, which caused Walter to laugh, but made her mother seethe. "I'm surprised you don't laugh at funerals, Walter," Ada complained.

"I might start. Those things are too dreary anyway," Walter quipped. "I guess I just never thought of it until you brought it up."

Walter seldom became miffed at any of his children, and he was delighted that his beautiful daughter was doing so well at Baylor and spreading her wings all the way up to Dallas. He expected great things from Maryon, and most of his children. When he looked up, Ada had stalked out of the room. She had immediately written a letter to Neiman-Marcus telling them not to charge any more dresses to Maryon.

A few days later, Walter paid the bill and enclosed a note asking the department store to keep his daughter's charges within reason. The bills from Neiman Marcus kept coming. And a couple of times, Walter thought that he needed to write his daughter a letter, making a casual point not to allow her weekends in Dallas to become a distraction from her studies. He had meant to but always managed to put the letter off.

So Walter was absolutely flabbergasted, when a telegram came from New York. Murphy and Maryon had been married by a justice of the peace in Dallas. They were honeymooning in New York, according to the wired message. "It's all your fault!" Ada shouted. Walter could not remember Ada ever screaming at him before. "You gave her too much rope and now she's hung herself with it," Ada charged. Now you get up to Dallas, Walter Oakley, and get that marriage annulled," she ordered.

None of the news from Dallas suited Ada at all. As Walter found out, Maryon did not need their permission to get married. She was past the legal age of consent. Almost as bad, Walter had to tell Ada that Mr. and Mrs. Murphy Webster, Sr. were delightful people, and even wealthier than Maryon's letters to Jimmie had claimed. They were ecstatic to have Maryon as their daughter-in-law and were buying a new house on Swiss Avenue for the newlyweds, when the couple returned from New York. "You'd really like them, Mother," Walter advanced tentatively.

"What I don't like is our daughter throwing away a brilliant future by marrying the first man she met after she left home," Ada fumed. "And I don't understand why you couldn't have the marriage annulled. She's just barely more than a schoolgirl."

"She's nineteen," Walter answered calmly, "and that's well past the age for a girl to consent to marriage." There were other things Walter could have said. The most important thing he did not tell his wife was something Murphy's father had said to him. When he heard Mr. Webster's words, Walter felt a cold shiver pass through his body. "We love Maryon, and we hope she'll settle Junior down," the banker had told Walter. A good marriage takes a lot of luck, Walter had often heard people say. That's what he wished for his daughter, but Murphy

Webster, Sr.'s words about his son settling down left a gnawing doubt Walter could not put aside.

If Ada and Walter had needed reminding that they had two grown daughters, the message was quickly delivered. Jimmie, like Maryon before her, could not wait to get away from Junction. She was on her way to San Antonio to attend business college two weeks after graduation. Walter asked some friends to keep an eye on his daughter, but Jimmie's hostility made it difficult for them to learn much. She almost never wrote, and even Maryon was concerned after she had received only one letter from her sister all summer. A letter from a high school friend who was a student at St. Mary's College in San Antonio prompted Maryon to act quickly. "I've got to go to San Antonio, and see about my sister," she told Murphy in October. Maryon felt apprehensive, when her husband did not offer to go with her, but she was too worried about Jimmie to wait. Maryon was on the first train south.

On her second night in San Antonio Maryon found her sister. Maryon's friend Elizabeth's warning had proved correct. Maryon learned just how true the report was, when she entered a speakeasy across the street from the Menger Hotel and walked up to Jimmie's table.

"Look what the cat drug in," Jimmie called out in a loud drunken slur, when she spotted Maryon. Reaching across the small marble-topped table, Maryon grabbed Jimmie's arm at the elbow.

"Time to go, little sister," the older Oakley daughter announced.

"Hey, who do you think you are anyway?" the drunken soldier sitting next to Jimmie protested, as he attempted unsuccessfully to stand.

"I'm this seventeen-year-old girl's big sister, Buster. And if you say one more word, I'm calling the cops, and filing rape charges on you," Maryon asserted.

"Ladies, how 'bout you move this disagreement outside, please?" the proprietor warned, walking around the bar and toward the table that Jimmie was clutching with both hands.

"Maybe I should call the cops on you, too," Maryon snapped at the barman. "You're serving illegal liquor to a minor."

Maryon had moved around the table to get a better grip on

Jimmie's arm. When Jimmie continued clinging to the table, Maryon used both hands to pry her loose. Jimmie held on tight, and the table overturned, sending ashtrays, and coffee cups containing liquor flying across the floor. The sound of police whistles was echoing up the sidewalk. Jimmie fought like a wildcat in a gunny sack, kicking and clawing the bartender with her nails. In spite of the scratches and bruises he was getting, he held Jimmie in a relentless grip until he reached the cabstand. Maryon held the door open on the side of the cab closest to the curb. While the barman kept Jimmie inside the car, Maryon rushed into the street and jumped through the opposite door. "I'm going to scratch your eyes out!" Jimmie screamed at the bartender, who was slamming the door and slapping the front door of the cab as a signal for the driver to pull away.

"Go!" the bartender ordered. "Keep your sister out of my place!" he hollered down the street at Maryon as the cab picked up speed. "I don't allow kids in here." The police arrived just as the bartender finished his last words.

"Looks like you got the worst of it, O'Brien," the first policeman taunted.

"I'll say," the second officer agreed, as he inspected the scratches on the man's face, and the blood on his shirt and apron.

Early the next evening when Maryon walked back into the speakeasy, O'Brien reached immediately for the phone.

"Operator, get me the police," he spoke urgently into the receiver. Then he turned to address Maryon. "I don't want any more trouble from you. My wife gave me the devil when I got home with all these cuts and scratches last night."

Maryon was quiet and demure as she walked over to the bar. "No more trouble," she said smiling. "I just want that soldier's name and address. I'm trying to find my sister. She ran off again," Maryon pleaded.

"Last favor," O'Brien responded, putting the telephone receiver back on the hook. He wrote the information on a blotter by the telephone, then tore a small piece of paper from the big sheet.

"Thank you," Maryon said as she turned to leave. "No more trouble from us," she called in parting.

It was early evening, and the address was only two blocks from the illegal gin joint. Maryon was shocked when she walked into the small room at the top of six flights of stairs. She knocked on the door, but no one answered. The door was cracked so Maryon pushed it open and walked inside. "Good God!" she exclaimed. Her sister and the soldier lay naked on top of the bed. The sheet was tangled, and an empty whiskey bottle rested on the floor beside the bed. The soldier snored loudly. Both of them were dead drunk.

Maryon went back to her hotel and ordered a bottle of Scotch brought up by room service. The porter bringing the whiskey looked suspiciously at her before handing over the bottle. "Will this do?" she asked, handing him a twenty-dollar bill. "Keep the change," Maryon concluded, closing the door.

She sat on her bed and cried for almost forty-five minutes before pouring some of the Scotch into a glass. After two or three sips, she reached for the phone and asked the operator to dial her new home on Swiss Avenue. "I'm afraid no one's answering," the long-distance operator said after several rings.

"Let it keep ringing, please?" Maryon begged. "I've just got to talk to my husband." The phone rang five more times before Murphy answered.

"Hello," he mumbled, sounding almost as drunk as the soldier Maryon had seen with her sister an hour earlier. Before she hung up the phone, Maryon heard the drunken laughter of a woman through the other end of the phone in Dallas. The Jazz Age had begun to lose its glitter for the disillusioned young honor student from Telegraph.

CHAPTER TWENTY-FOUR

"Hello mother," Jimmie called from the platform as Ada stepped off the train. Ada was both relieved and alarmed.

"You look better," Ada said, as mother and daughter hugged just beyond the cloud of steam covering the space between the platform and the passenger coach. "You're not as skinny as last time," Ada told her.

"Oh Mother," Jimmie responded, laughing and hugging her mother a second time. Ada was alarmed by the excessively heavy amount of makeup her daughter was wearing. Her lips were blazing red. Rouge glowed on her cheeks, and her face was heavily powdered. Not ordinarily reticent, Ada fought her impulse to say something about the face paint. Ada held her tongue, trying hard not to begin the visit badly.

"You look very nice," Ada said carefully, if not candidly. "I hope you're not spending all your money on clothes."

"Is that the first thing you say to Maryon when you see her?" Jimmie challenged.

"Yes," Ada admitted with a smile. In a few minutes. Jimmie and Ada were standing beside a new Chevrolet convertible.

"Just put them in the back," Jimmie directed the redcap carrying her mother's bags.

"This isn't yours!" Ada exclaimed, while staring at the new car in disbelief.

"Of course not, Mother," Jimmie laughed as she opened the passenger door for her mother. "Mr. Alsop just let me borrow it to come pick you up," Jimmie laughed again, noting the relief on her mother's face. Ada was not reassured. She smelled the same odor she had noticed when she first hugged Jimmie on the platform. The car and her daughter both smelled like cigars.

"Here," Ada said, passing a dime to Jimmie. "That's for the porter," she explained.

"Mother, I already gave him a quarter," Jimmie told Ada, gently pushing her mother's hand away.

"I'd like to know where you girls get all your money," Ada declared, unable to hide her concern. "Well Mother, I work for mine," Jimmie answered. "And the last time I heard, my sister's father-in-law still owned a bank." Jimmie was laughing, hoping to get her mother to relax.

"I suppose I still haven't gotten used to these things," Ada sighed, her voice sounding far away.

As they drove, Jimmie was constantly pointing in almost every direction. "That's the new Joske's," she began.

"I'm glad you're driving," Ada remarked with a chuckle. "I hardly recognize anything. San Antonio's gotten so big, I'm afraid I would have gotten lost."

Jimmie smiled. "I'm glad I'm driving, too," she agreed, laughing again. "From what Dad tells me, you still don't know how to drive."

Ada pretended to scold her daughter. "I'm going to surprise you one of these days. I'll come driving into town all by myself and just knock right on your door." Mother and daughter laughed the rest of the way to Jimmie's new apartment.

"This is it," Jimmie announced, as she parked the Chevrolet in front of the building. It was a single story and shaped in the form of a square. The front was a Spanish style wall facing the street. The wall partially revealed a landscaped courtyard. The exterior of the buildings, and the wall that enclosed the apartments, were whitewashed stucco. The roof was red tile. Ada was looking busily in all directions as they walked under the arched, wrought iron gateway through the wall.

"I don't see how you can afford to live in a place like this," Jimmie said in perfect imitation of her mother, anticipating what was coming next.

"Well I don't," Ada protested, while attempting a smile that appeared, but seemed incompletely honest.

"Mother, my rent is twenty-two dollars and seventy-five cents a month. The place is safe, and right on the streetcar line to work. I bought these clothes last Saturday so I would have something nice to wear when I picked you up at the depot. "Now please tell me that we are not going to spend your whole visit here talking about money. I work hard. I'm a bookkeeper and secretary for Alsop Chevrolet. And thanks to your insistence, I finished my business course at Austin Business College," Jimmie said as she paused to unlock the door of her apartment.

"You promised, Mother," Jimmie continued as the two walked into Jimmie's small combination living room-dining area.

"I know I did," Ada confessed. "I'm sorry. I've been doing my best not to ask all these questions, but I'll try harder." Ada attempted to keep a conciliatory expression on her face, but she was extremely concerned. The cigar odor inside Jimmie's apartment was even stronger than it had been on the train platform, and in the borrowed Chevrolet. "Where's the bathroom?" Ada asked quickly. "I need to wash my face."

Ada was not good at pretending, but it was important that she and Jimmie get back on a solid footing. Her daughter needed her. And as Walter had pointed out more than once, Ada could not hope to help Jimmie with her problems, if the two were not speaking. Ada's estrangement from Jimmie had been the longest nine months of her life. Ada had been back from San Antonio four days before Ada and Walter sat alone on their front porch to talk about her visit. Walter rocked quietly as he listened to his wife list the things she had observed that made her believe Jimmie was having an illicit relationship with her boss.

"I suspected the same," Walter admitted after a long silence. "But I don't know what we can do about it. It's not what I want for our daughter, Mother. Please don't take what I'm about to say the wrong way," Walter continued. "But the fact is, since Maryon's visit to San Antonio and the showdown you had with Jimmie after that, things have gotten better."

"I don't see how you can say sleeping with a married man at a place that he pays for is better," Ada interrupted.

"Like I said," Walter resumed. His voice was even, but the expression on his face urged his wife not to interrupt. "It's not what I want for Jimmie, but it's better than staying drunk with some soldier twice her age half the time. She did finish business school before she left San Antonio. She does have a job, even if that is part of her problem. And she hasn't had any more trouble with the police." Ada was not convinced, but she sat silently thinking of what Walter had just said. "It's hard to accept, but things have been much worse. Maybe she'll grow out of this. I just don't know," Walter finally admitted.

"I hope you're right," Ada conceded after a long quiet interval. "I want you to be right, but Glenn never grew out of his drinking problems. I just can't stand to see Jimmie going down the same road."

Taking Ada's hand, her husband expressed his agreement, "I know Mother. You said that you were sure Jimmie wasn't drinking while you were there. Five days is a long time. Maybe there is hope."

Ada repeated her pronouncement, after another silence. "Yes Walter, there is always hope."

But both parents knew they were grasping at any possibility of positive change that could be uttered in support of their daughter who seemed almost certainly to be lost.

Jimmie met Maryon's train in Houston much the way she had her mother's in San Antonio. The months between those two visits had been distressing for both sisters. "You look beautiful!" Maryon raved as she embraced Jimmie.

"You don't look bad yourself, kid," Jimmie responded.

"You mean I don't look divorced," Maryon countered.

"Have you told mother yet?" Jimmie asked.

"I don't know how," Maryon confessed.

"I'm sure Dad told her all my bad news for me," Jimmie offered.

"She hasn't written yet?" Maryon asked, as the two young women summoned a redcap, and began rounding up Maryon's luggage.

"Yes, she wrote, but she didn't ask anything about what happened in San Antonio, and she didn't mention Lewis either. The letter was mostly encouragement on what a promising future I have ahead of me. I put it in the drawer with all the others," Jimmie admitted. Her voice began to crack with emotion as she fished in her purse for a cigarette.

"Now don't be too hard on Mother," Maryon continued. "She only wants what's best for you, and she loves you very much. Besides you must admit ..." Jimmie cut her off.

"You don't have to tell me that my mother loves me. I may be a drunk and a fool, but I still know about my own mother. If you're going to start this, get yourself back on that train!" Jimmie fumed.

"I'm sorry," Maryon apologized, her tone gentle and empathetic. "I didn't come to tell you how to run your life. I came because I've made such a disaster of my own. I need your help," Maryon said, collapsing onto a bench standing against the wall of the station. She was sobbing and hid her face in a handkerchief.

"It's all right, Sis," Jimmie soothed, sitting down beside Maryon, and cradling her with her left arm. "No man is worth all the tears you have cried over that useless cheat," Jimmie charged. While she listened to Maryon cry, Jimmie thought back to the letters Maryon had written, when she had first met Murphy. *What was I so jealous of?* Jimmie wondered in disbelief. *Was I afraid my sister would mess up her whole life before I had a chance to ruin my own?* Jimmie looked at the porter who was standing patiently and discreetly about fifty feet from the unhappy sisters. She motioned for him to come over and gently pressed a quarter into his hand.

"She's trying so hard to impress you," Lewis attempted to explain to Maryon, later that evening after Jimmie had gone to bed. "This is the very first night since I met her that Jimmie didn't have a drink."

Maryon was agitated and appeared not to be paying attention. "I'd like one," she snapped, clearly wary of this latest in a growing list of older men who had come into Jimmie's life.

"Sure," Lewis responded. "I think I'll join you for a quick drink. Then I'll leave." They sat for a few minutes staring over their glasses at one another. "I'm really not a bad person," he offered to no reaction from Maryon at all. "I got along very well with your father," Lewis tried after a silent interlude.

"Dad can get along with anyone," Maryon challenged. "I wouldn't put too much hope in that, if I were you."

Lewis was frustrated. "Can't you see how much I love your sister?" he pleaded.

"I'm not even sure I know what love is," Maryon answered, surprising herself at being so revealing to a stranger. "I'm sorry," Maryon said after another silence. "This is all so awkward. I know my father came to see about Jimmie, and I had gathered that he spent some time with you, but you are really mostly a stranger to me. "I came to Houston to talk to my sister—not about you, and certainly not about my own problems. I don't want to seem rude, but I've just been through too many awful experiences of my own to focus on someone else's trouble. "I guess it's really silly of me to lean on Jimmie, though. Whatever I've had to deal with, she's had much worse. Please forgive me?" Maryon finished.

"I love Jimmie like I've never loved any other person in my whole life," Lewis explained, as he rose to his feet. "I want to marry her, and I want her family to accept that marriage." Maryon was stunned by Lewis' sincerity.

"You're a man old enough ... " Maryon began, then abruptly stopped.

"To be her father?" Lewis finished her sentence. "Old enough to know better, even old enough to have the judgment and self-restraint not to take advantage of a young girl so battered and vulnerable. Yes, all those things are true," Lewis acknowledged.

"If you know all those things, and if you really love Jimmie, why are you so insistent that she marry you?" Maryon asked quietly.

"To save her from herself," Lewis answered. "If she goes on drifting the way she has been, she'll be dead in two years. I couldn't stand myself if I let that happen."

"I need to talk to my sister before I say anything else," Maryon responded evenly. "But I'll try my best to give you a chance. I'll get to know you better before I make a final judgment about you. And that's a big concession coming from a member of my family."

CHAPTER TWENTY-FIVE

The next evening Lewis insisted that Jimmie and Maryon go to dinner without him. He wanted the two sisters to have an opportunity to talk without constraint. Jimmie and Maryon were the only women in the diner Jimmie had picked.

"It always rains in Houston," she lamented. "I don't think I'll ever get used to that. Thanks for coming out with me. I just couldn't stand cooking again. I've been cooped up in that apartment too much."

Maryon had been dying to get her younger sister alone so she could find out what had gone so seriously wrong that Jimmie felt she had to move to Houston.

"Why did you leave San Antonio?" Maryon asked.

"My boss' wife," Jimmie replied. "I think she might have killed both of us, if I hadn't left. I was pretty ashamed after Momma's visit ended, and she went back home. Look, I just don't know. I don't know why I do most of the stupid things I do."

Maryon took her sister's hand. Jimmie was near tears.

"It's none of my business," Maryon said. "I'm just trying to figure out what's going on—not just with you, but with myself, and with almost everyone I know. "You won't believe this, but I want to move back home with Mother and Dad. It seems like they're the only sane people I've ever known," Maryon confessed.

Jimmie agreed. "I know exactly what you mean. But I just couldn't wait to get out of there. I was so jealous when you got to go away to college."

"I really messed that up," Maryon conceded sadly.

"Oh, I wasn't talking about you. I was talking about how silly I was, when you went away to school. I just wanted to be older, and smarter, and pretty like you," Jimmie explained.

Now Maryon was holding both of her sister's hands, hoping that Jimmie would not cry.

"Wouldn't it be funny?" Jimmie suggested with a conspiratorial laugh. "The two of us living back in Junction, the fallen sisters of two notorious bootleggers?"

It wasn't funny at all. It was heartbreakingly sad, but Maryon laughed anyway. When the food came, it was Maryon's turn to contribute to the women's despair.

"That's the worst part of it," Maryon explained. "I can't go home, because my being divorced would be such an embarrassment to our family. I don't think anyone in Junction has ever been divorced."

Jimmie agreed again. "You're probably right. But if you think you messed things up at college, why not go back to Baylor?" Jimmie noted that Maryon was deeply sad, when she spoke.

"I can't. They won't let me come back because I'm divorced."

"Baptists!" Jimmie spat, "minding everybody's business but their own."

There were so many things Maryon wanted to tell her sister. She wanted to talk about how her marriage had gone wrong; about how understanding her in-laws had been; about how wonderful their father had been, consoling and so understanding.

"Is there somewhere else you can go to school?" Jimmie asked.

"I think my mother-in-law is looking into that," Maryon answered. "She's so sorry about how things turned out. She even said they would pay for me to finish my education. The trouble is, I just don't know what I want to do. Sometimes I think I want to erase everything that happened and start again. And other times, I look back at all the fun

Murphy and I had, and how exciting it was. When I think about those things, I long to have it all back."

Jimmie understood her sister's urge to erase her mistakes, but she had never experienced the romance and excitement that Maryon had. For Jimmie, all her encounters with men amounted to a list of souls who were just as desperate as Jimmie was. And each new man she had collected had been discovered while Jimmie and her new companion were both dead drunk—at least everyone but Lewis.

When Jimmie had met Lewis, she had been so drunk that she had passed out right after the two had left a speakeasy. Jimmie no longer remembered the name of the place where she had been drinking. She hadn't even remembered meeting Lewis. In Jimmie's first memory of Lewis, she had been on her knees in vomit-soaked clothes. Her arms had been wrapped around an unfamiliar toilet, and Lewis had been standing beside her holding a wet washcloth on the back of her neck. After each new wave of vomiting passed, Lewis would refold the washcloth and wipe the residue from Jimmie's face, neck, and chest. Lewis had been attempting to take care of Jimmie ever since that first memory. He definitely drank too much, but his intake of liquor paled in comparison with Jimmie's.

"How did we get like this?" Jimmie wondered aloud. "It all happened so fast."

At home along the South Llano River, Ada and Walter prayed, worried and agonized over what possible solution to their troubled family's problems they might be overlooking.

Part Three
$1,000 FOR BROUSSARD'S 8 CHILDREN

CHAPTER TWENTY-SIX

Ada had more than her share of heartaches, and she seemed to always be plagued by a cloud of worries about her children. Even so, except for Glenn's death, nothing had hurt Ada more than Ralph's failure to learn from his younger brother's tragic life and early end. No matter how many years had passed, Ada could not escape the torment she had suffered only months after Glenn's murder when Ralph had jumped right back into a life of crime. That awful man Fernando Ortiz might have fled to Cuba, but he, or some other criminal master just like him, had come back into her oldest son's life, tempting him with another phony promise of wealth. This was the way Ada had imagined Ralph's return to crime in a new location five-hundred miles to the north and east of Matamoros in Louisiana. She saw these scenes repeat over and over in her nightmares.

In these lifelike visions, Ada was horrified as she was compelled to watch everything from a seemingly hidden vantage point. She was powerless to intervene or communicate in any way as Ralph peeled some bills and stepped onto the deck of the *Sonya Marie*. The Cajun accepted the money, folded it, and put it in his pocket. "Broussard," the captain called out. "Emile Broussard," the Cajun added, extending his hand to greet Ralph. "Ralph Oakley," Ralph reciprocated, thrusting his hand forward to meet Emile's—and an instant later, remembering to smile. Emile motioned to a pile of shrimp nets on the deck. "Have a seat," he invited, laughing. "Anywhere you like. And I'll get us underway."

Seconds after Emile turned from Ralph, the lines were loosed, the two-cylinder gasoline engine burped to life and began bumping and shaking the boat. Emile engaged the prop and edged the throttle up. The *Sonya Marie* began pushing through the heavy bayou water and into the channel. Emile gave a blast on the horn for good measure. Once he had the *Sonya Marie* headed toward the gulf, Emile turned to Ralph. "Not that it matters, but where you from?" the shrimper asked. "Telegraph," Ralph answered, remembering to keep the tone in his voice friendly just before he spoke. The answer surprised Ralph. It was true of course, but it was an answer he never gave. Ralph's usual reply was St. Louis which sounded more important. Or sometimes he simply said Texas.

"Where's that?' Emile asked.

"Out west of San Antonio," Ralph replied, still wondering why he had spoken aloud the name of a place that wasn't at all important—a place where weak people, people like his father, not powerful men like Ralph Oakley—lived. Ralph needed to be someplace powerful. Then he laughed inside his head. Powerful? Ralph thought about where he was at the moment, some no place on the Texas-Louisiana border. Ralph was just beginning to enjoy the irony, a rare if not unique experience for him, when he heard Emile's voice again.

"Why you come all this way to go fishing and don't bring no fishing pole?" the keen-witted Cajun challenged. Ralph smiled, then laughed aloud and good-naturedly.

"Ole Emile, he guesses maybe you want to find some special kind of fish, huh? Maybe you want to find where to meet some of those fish that have been coming over here from Cuba?" Emile teased.

The tour lasted twelve hours. Emile showed Ralph hundreds of inlets, small islands, and coves. The Louisiana coast had an endless supply of places to hide. There was no way to secure it against smugglers. Emile talked, and asked questions the entire time that the pair of conspirators was on the water. Ralph quickly learned that he did not have to answer Emile's questions or even participate in the conversation. For Emile, talking was as involuntary as breathing. When Ralph did not respond to his questions, Emile made up his own answers. Sometimes they were right, and sometimes not. It really didn't matter to Emile. His mouth was like an open faucet draining thoughts from his hyperactive brain. Ralph supposed that Emile likely talked in his sleep. Ordinarily, Ralph would have been irritated far past his point of distraction by behavior like Emile's, but Ralph recognized that this illiterate Cajun fisherman had talents that would help make Ralph rich.

It was after ten o'clock that night, when Emile backed the *Sonya Marie* into her slip. Ralph wished to demonstrate that he was grateful for the shrimper's help. Before he stepped from the boat, he handed Emile another one-hundred fifty dollars. "I'll see you in a few days," Ralph informed his newfound accomplice.

"I'll be right here," Emile pledged.

Ralph was tempted to drive all the way to New Orleans that night, but he decided to return to the tourist court in Lake Charles where he had slept the previous night. His sleep had been fitful, and Ralph was speeding toward New Orleans just after sunup. Two afternoons later, Emile was waiting for Ralph, who had forgotten about his self-professed decision to treat Emile with patience and deference. Ralph barreled aboard the shrimp boat and snapped, "Let's get going, or we're gonna be late."

"Good afternoon to you, too," Emile responded cheerfully, and kept on with his preparations to get under way. "Late for what?" the Cajun called out.

"We need to meet someone," Ralph answered with growing impatience, while pulling a cigar from his jacket. Emile's smile disappeared.

"This someone wouldn't have a boat load of liquor, would they?" Emile asked.

"Well of course they do," Ralph grumped. "Don't pretend like you believe I gave you all that money for a boat ride."

"You're not putting any liquor on the *Sonya Marie*," Emile announced with conviction.

"What's the matter? Hundred dollars a trip not enough for you?" Ralph challenged.

"Oh, it's plenty. But you ain't puttin' no liquor on this boat."

Ralph continued in a calmer tone of voice. "So, what's the problem then? And don't tell me you got something against liquor?"

Emile was calm, but he did not smile. "No, I like to drink liquor just fine," he replied.

"Then what?" Ralph repeated.

"Two things: the guys with the liquor got too many guns, and the Coast Guard got even more and bigger guns," Emile continued. "Now me, I got a gun. But I only use my gun to hunt ducks. I'm not gonna get myself killed over no whiskey."

Ralph's face turned crimson, and he chomped hard on his cigar before he spoke. "You knew what I wanted when you took me out. Why did you take my money, if you weren't going to help, if you didn't want to make some real money?" Ralph asked, as he envisioned the first big liquor deal he had set up on his own blowing up, and his earnest money being flushed away right along with it.

"Now hold on," Emile urged. "I didn't say I wasn't going to help you. I just said you couldn't put no liquor on this boat."

"What do you mean?" Ralph demanded.

"It means you need a speedboat," Emile grinned.

"How much?" Ralph barked.

"Oh, I think Ozio's got one you can get for seven hundred. Real fast, too," Emile smiled.

"Seven hundred?" Ralph screamed. "That's more than I'm making on this whole deal. If I have to pay seven hundred dollars a trip, I'll be out of business in less than a month."

Emile roared with laughter. "Not seven hundred a trip. Seven hundred to buy," he managed.

"Well how do I make the rendezvous?" Ralph asked, beginning to calm.

"You hire Emile," the shrimper explained. "I'll lead you out, and I'll lead you back in. When we get in sight of shore, I'll point the way. You give it the gas and you're home free. And if the Coast Guard shows up, you make a run for it, and I keep 'em busy. Not bad for a hundred bucks, huh?" Emile beamed.

The deep color of outrage had disappeared from Ralph's face. "Let's find Ozio," Ralph commanded. "We're late."

In less than twenty minutes, Ralph in his new speedboat, and Emile aboard the *Sonya Marie*, were headed into the gulf. As soon as they cleared the jetties, the eighteen-foot speedboat began to plunge into the troughs of the swells, then fall off the wave tops nose first. For fifteen minutes, Ralph was certain he was going to drown. But gradually he began to get used to the roller coaster and decided he probably would live. Every now and then, Emile would look back, flash his snaggle-toothed smile, and wave just as Ralph's boat fell from the peak of another giant swell, watching with amusement as Ralph held on to the steering wheel for all he was worth. Each time the speedboat crashed down from a wave, walls of solid water rose eight or ten feet above the small craft on both sides. Eventually, as Ralph began to adapt by watching what Emile was doing to navigate the massive swells, the boats became synchronized with the tumultuous sea. And their forward speed, dictated by the much slower shrimp boat, was just fast enough so that the water did not fall back into Ralph's zippy little vessel. Ralph's tailored suit fared less well. His clothes were drenched by heavy spray from the swells. As the boat was tossed and thrown about, Ralph tried to figure out why men wasted money buying boats to sail out into the Gulf of Mexico. For Ralph, what was happening amounted to torture, and this boat ride was anything but fun. In three-and-a-half-hours, the skillful Emile maneuvered the two boats to a spot twelve miles from the coast. The twilight was fading when Ralph noticed Emile waving to get his attention. Ralph concentrated on what the sea was doing to his boat, while struggling to keep an eye on Emile. Finally Ralph's eyes homed in on a faint shape between the swells that Emile was pointing out. It was the silhouette of a small freighter, shrouded by spray, about a mile ahead. For ten more minutes, the two small boats dived off the crests, progressing slowly toward the little Cuban ship. Then Emile began waving again. Half-a-mile to the right of the vessel they were to meet, wallowing in the sea but moving toward Ralph and Emile, was a Coast Guard patrol boat.

Ralph followed Emile when he turned back toward Cameron. As Ralph brought his tiny craft about, a wave broke over him, nearly swallowing the speedboat. Indeed, Ralph found it was far more difficult to keep his new boat from swamping with the swells pursuing than it had been when they were sailing into the breaking waves. Each time he would ride up over the top of a swell, the water would shoot him forward. However, when his trip to the top of a wave was ill timed and caught the breaking swell, water cascaded into the boat. It seemed to Ralph that he was in danger of sinking and he decided he had to do something to avoid running up on the curls. Emile was operating without lights. After Ralph throttled back, he found it difficult to keep Emile in view as the growing darkness settled over the gulf. For his part, Emile was determined not to let the Coast Guard catch the two small boats. He had nothing to hide, but he didn't want the patrol boat to get close enough to identify the *Sonya Marie*.

About three miles from Calcasieu Pass, the sea calmed, Emile switched on his running lights and began circling as he waited for Ralph to catch up. Twenty minutes passed before Ralph spotted the lights on the shrimp boat. When Emile was certain Ralph had found him, the little Cajun stopped circling and set a course straight for the pass. Ralph did not become convinced he was going to survive until the two boats were safely on the brown waters of Calcasieu Lake, where the waves were less than a foot high. Emile led Ralph to the slip where he would dock the *Sonya Marie* and signaled for Ralph to hold back. When his boat was secure, Emile waved his hand as a sign that Ralph should ease his speedboat up to the dock. Emile took the line from the bow, pulled the boat up, and helped Ralph onto the pier. Handing the line to Ralph, Emile picked up a small pirogue, which had been resting upside down on the dock, and launched it beside the speedboat. Then he took the line from Ralph, got in the speedboat and maneuvered it to a spot about fifteen feet in front of the *Sonya Marie*, where he dropped an anchor into the gray mud on the lake bottom.

"You don't owe me any money until we bring some whiskey back," Emile told Ralph. "I get paid by the load, not by the trip." Ralph was not sure there would be any more trips. He drove his new Ford as fast as he could over the bumpy shell road toward Lake Charles. The temperature of the moist gulf air was still about eighty degrees, but Ralph was freezing, riding in the open car wearing wet clothes. He was too tired to eat when he returned to the tourist court and fell onto the bed in his still partially wet clothes and probably ruined shoes, but he didn't fall asleep. In about forty minutes, Ralph walked to the pay phone that hung on the outside wall of the motel office. The man on the other end of Ralph's phone call to New Orleans told him that the ship would be waiting for him at a new location the next evening and gave Ralph the coordinates.

Emile could not read and had no sea charts. But by dusk the next day, he had led Ralph through much calmer waters to within a mile of the ship. It was there, and so was the Coast Guard. Because the seas were much calmer, Emile motioned for Ralph to pull up beside the *Sonya Marie*. "I can't outrun the patrol boat in calm seas, so I'm going to drop my nets and begin dragging for shrimp between you and the Coast Guard. You make a run for it," Emile said. Ralph had no trouble outrunning the patrol boat and this time the water did not wash into his boat.

However, Ralph had no sense of direction in the dark. In less than an hour, he spotted the shadowed outline of the Louisiana shore. As he throttled back the highly powered boat, Ralph watched as his skin seemed to disappear behind an almost solid curtain of mosquitoes which had buzzed in from the marsh, seeking a meal of human blood. For an hour, Ralph cruised slowly back and forth searching for Calcasieu Pass. Eventually, he concluded that he had come too far west, so he navigated about five-hundred yards away from the shoreline, deeper into the gulf, in a vain effort to escape the mosquitoes. Ralph sailed east along the coast until almost ten o'clock, when he spotted an inlet that appeared promising. Once inside, it became clear the opening was not Calcasieu Pass, but a much shorter cut into a different bay or lake. He was exhausted and almost out of gas. He took refuge from the mosquitoes by wrapping himself head to toe in a canvas cockpit cover specially designed for his boat. The cocoon he had fashioned was miserably hot, but it probably constituted a better survival strategy than remaining at the mercy of the endless swarms of mosquitoes.

A short time before sunrise, Ralph heard small shrimp boats chugging into what he would learn was Vermilion Bay. He ate breakfast offered by a local shrimper and got his boat fueled. Ralph obtained directions back to Cameron from the shrimper who had cooked breakfast for him. Three hours later, he was back in Cameron.

Despite his difficult start, Ralph quickly became a successful small-time rumrunner. Twice a week, Emile led him to a rendezvous with a small ship or yacht, hovering off the coast in international waters, loaded with liquor. When Ralph's speedboat was packed with illegal alcohol, Emile would lead him back to safety. Ralph's pile of money from smuggling grew rapidly, and the bootlegging runs became routine until one night in November, just over a year after Ralph and Emile's first encounter. That night, there was a light fog partially obscuring the calm surface of the sea thirteen miles off Cameron. The spot was clearly in international waters. When the Coast Guard opened fire, Ralph gunned his engine and began racing further into the gulf at full speed. He was completely certain there had been no warning announcement, no searchlight, nothing—just the terrifying rattle of machine gun fire through the fog.

Ralph ran full out for five minutes, then slowed, and cut his engine to listen. Silence. Ralph guessed that he had stopped perhaps two to three miles from where the gunfire had erupted. He sat totally quiet and completely still for twenty minutes, hoping to hear the distinct sound of the engine that powered the *Sonya Marie*. Eventually, Ralph gave up and motored west toward the Texas coast, maintaining a deliberately slow pace, hoping that he would be able to hear any noise made by the engine from any nearby vessel. But so far as Ralph could tell, he was all alone in this stretch of the Gulf of Mexico. When the young bootlegger spotted the sweeping beam from the lighthouse positioned at the end of the Port Arthur Jetty, he changed course, allowing his boat to pass just offshore from Texas Point. Then, he followed the Texas coastline to a spot half-a-mile west of High Island. Ralph recalled having seen a small service station combined with a general store beside the beach road there, perhaps three hundred yards from the water's edge. A payphone was attached to the side wall on the outside of the small, weathered building. Without so much as hello, Ralph began speaking to the person who answered the phone in New Orleans. "We had a big problem tonight. My guide and I got separated. What do you know?"

"Nothing good," the unidentified voice answered, "but we can't talk on this line. Give me five minutes, and call back on the alternate phone," Ralph was told. "A stray round from a machine gun killed our friend," the mystery voice at the other end of the phone reported during the second call. "Cool off for a few days," the contact advised. "We'll talk later." Ralph heard a click, then a dial tone. He hung up the phone and returned to the speedboat.

Four days later, Ralph made another call from an outdoor payphone at a fishing camp near Palacios, Texas—far from Cameron—where the young fugitive had gone to ground. This time, the contact was at another payphone some distance from his own business. That telephone was outside a bar on Decatur Street in New Orleans' French Quarter. Ralph learned that Emile had died instantly, slumping to the deck of the *Sonya Marie*, a boat that had never carried a drop of illegal alcohol. "What do you want to do?" the voice asked Ralph.

"I've got a new plan. I want you to get someone to put a thousand dollars in cash in a bag and leave that bag in a locker inside Southern Pacific Depot in Lake Charles. Mail the key to the widow," Ralph directed.

"Done," the voice affirmed. "Call when you're ready to go back to work." And once again, the phone went dead.

At the Oakley home in Telegraph, Ada and Walter, Ralph's parents, were worried sick that a second of their sons had been killed in the war between the smugglers of illegal alcohol, and the federal cops, who made no secret of their purpose. They intended to kill as many bootleggers as they could. And they had convinced themselves that they had the support of the American people to use lethal force any time, and under whatever circumstances they decided were appropriate.

With Emile dead, Ralph stopped running liquor by boat and learned a few basics of flying an airplane. On his third aerial adventure, he crash-landed his small biplane on Pecan Island, Louisiana, later learning that federal agents had been tracking his flights. The revenue men were quite close to the crash site, and they had Ralph in custody only minutes after he freed himself from the cockpit. Rumors circulated around the federal lockup inside the Old Mint in New Orleans indicating that the feds might even have sabotaged Ralph's plane, but Ralph's lawyer was unable to find any proof of those rumors that might have nullified his client's arrest. The attorney lived in Lake Charles and had come to visit Ralph in jail after being contacted by one of Ralph's New Orleans associates. The lawyer's name was O'Neal, and he had gone to Tulane Law School, and roomed with a young man with a strange first name, Oramel. The roommates shared a keen interest in politics. By the time Ralph and O'Neal met at the lockup inside the New Orleans Mint, the roommate was much better known than his old law school chum. That's because by then, the former roommate had become Governor Oramel Simpson.

Neither Ralph nor his attorney would ever reveal the details, but Ralph promised to pay every dime he had made during his Louisiana bootlegging days, and all charges were dismissed. Ralph walked out of the federal building a free man, but penniless. He wired his Uncle Sid in St. Louis, asking for train fare. He'd had to send the telegram collect, meaning that Ralph's uncle had to pay for it before it could be delivered to him.

Walter Oakley had learned from a longtime friend, a Texas Ranger assigned to San Antonio, that his oldest son had been arrested. He began his search in Lake Charles and learned that Ralph had taken a shrimper in the coastal community of Cameron as a partner. Just as Ralph had done, Walter drove to the little village and learned from several of the shrimp fishermen about the handsome, spiffily dressed young man who had appeared on the dock more than a year before. He had worn a yellow, hand-tailored three-piece suit with white spats and expensive shoes, polished to a mirror sheen. The boatmen told Walter that the man they had seen had driven a new Ford that still had a paper dealer tag issued in Texas. The man smoked a cigar and acted overly friendly. He had clearly been in a hurry. One of the shrimpers told Walter that the young man produced a large roll of bills, and said he wanted to hire a boat for the day. That same man related that a shrimper named Emile Broussard had made a deal with the stranger, and that deal had apparently been the cause of Broussard's untimely death. The helpful shrimper had shaken his head and looked down into the murky bayou. "His wife was pregnant, and he left seven little children with no daddy. Damn feds even took his shrimp boat. Poor lady got nothin'," the man said.

Part Four
SHATTERED DREAMS

CHAPTER TWENTY-SEVEN

Brooks Oakley's dreams were huge. His dreams became goals, and he learned how to plan meticulously so that they would come true. Brooks was a dreamer who accomplished his life's goals using an iron will and working harder than everyone else—not just most of the time, but all of the time. Because he was a dreamer, he seldom acknowledged that there were unknowable things and events in everyone's life. As his high school education was ending, Brooks had no way of knowing that reality was about to smash into him with the fury of a Hill Country flash flood. When that harsh dose of reality struck, Brooks Oakley was forced to reflect back to determine what had gone wrong. He had planned so carefully, beginning before he graduated to high school from eighth grade.

As part of Brooks' extended eighth-grade graduation celebration, the students from Telegraph were treated to a bus ride to Junction, and a picnic with the eighth graders at the county's other school, the one in Junction. The trip, and the merging of the students from the county's two primary schools was intended to be a social gathering, but the city kids from Junction looked down on their cousins from the country. There was never any chance that the picnic would meld the two groups into one before they entered Kimble County's only high school in Junction the next fall. After lunch, the boys were scheduled to have a tug of war, then a softball game. There were more boys from the Junction school. They also were, by and large, bigger than the country kids, so the tug of war was no contest. The taunting of the kids from Telegraph escalated so quickly that the Junction principal, who was also the football coach, decided to step in. "All right," Coach Shiflet interjected into the scuffling and verbal disparagement that was quickly growing out of control. "Everyone settle down. Maybe, before we start the softball game, we should have a relay race." The coach had heard that some of the boys from Telegraph were fast runners, and he hoped a win or a strong showing by the rural kids might even things out and perhaps diminish the animosity between the two groups.

"The boys from Junction get over here," he directed from the shade of a giant live oak he sheltered under. "And I want the boys from the Telegraph school to get together under that tree, there," Principal Shiflet instructed, pointing at another live oak of nearly equal size. "Each school is to pick your four fastest sprinters," the coach concluded. His quickly devised diversion prevented a fight from breaking out between the two groups of boys. Immediately, arguing began within each knot about which four boys were fastest. Coach Shiflet allowed three minutes for the selections. "Have you made your choices?" he asked in a loud voice. In a short time, the fastest four boys were pushed out of each of the two clusters. Each newly selected team stood sheepishly in front of their school groups. None of the youngsters understood what a relay race was, but they were eager for competition. The girls had also formed two groups apart from each other, a few of them giggling in nervous anticipation of this new experience in their young lives.

"In a relay race, each of the four men runs the same distance. I'm going to walk off four segments, each of fifty yards. I'll place a rock to mark the segments each individual competitor will run. "The first man will begin at the starting and finish line, run fifty yards, and hand his stick to the second man on his team waiting at the first rock," the confident new authority, who had just become part of these young people's lives, explained in a voice strong enough for everyone to hear. "The second man will hand the stick to the third man at the next rock, and the third man will hand the stick to the fourth man waiting at the last rock. You should save your fastest man for the final fifty yards." The boys enjoyed hearing the coach call them men, and waves of excitement crackled like electrical charges through both groups. The boys from Junction were sure they would win, and the boys from Telegraph were looking for a chance to get even. The tension within the youngsters soared, as Coach Shiflet began pacing off the course, and placing the rocks.

As the runners reported to their positions around the course, the excitement felt unbearable. Coach Shiflet had a whistle around his neck that he would use to signal the start of the race. The boys from Telegraph had never been around anything that seemed so official. "On your marks. Get set," Coach Shiflet barked. And when the whistle trilled shrilly, Lynn Hardy exploded off the starting line for the Telegraph team, seemingly stunning his competitor. In a heartbeat, Lynn had passed the stick into the hands of Robert Rienstrau, who was nearly to the third runner before the first contestant from Junction handed his stick to his teammate. The race took the appearance of being no contest at all. Rienstrau put the makeshift baton into the hand of Jake Doornbos, as Brooks waited impatiently. Doornbos was a fast runner, but clumsy. Brooks looked over his shoulder as the Junction stick was passed to their third runner. A broad smile came to his face, but it disappeared a second later, when Jake tripped on a rock. His chin struck the ground, and it appeared he was out cold. Brooks was about to run to pick up Jake's stick, when he heard the coach's voice. "Leave him alone. Each man must run his own leg," Mr. Shiflet called.

The runner from Junction was now approaching his teammate who stood poised near Brooks. Jake had stumbled to his feet, and was moving toward Brooks groggily, just as Junction's fastest runner took the stick. By the time Telegraph's wand was passed from Jake to Brooks, the Junction anchorman was halfway to the finish line, running full out. All across the field, mouths fell wide open as Brooks streaked over the finish line two full steps ahead of the runner from Junction. Half a minute passed before there was any sound but the runners gasping for breath. Finally, Coach Shiflet's strong voice boomed over the sports grounds. "The winner," he proclaimed, before dramatically pausing for effect. "Telegraph!"

The boys and girls from the south end of the county shrieked. Brooks' astounding performance had carried the day. No one there, including Coach Shiflet, who had trained high school athletes his whole life, had ever seen anything like it. The next Friday, there was a note waiting for Brooks at school. Coach Shiflet had asked Brooks' principal if Brooks could come to Junction after lunch that day to work out with the football team. As he read the note, Brooks screamed for joy inside his head. His dream was coming true! In the afternoon, Brooks' principal drove his honored student to Junction. After everyone was assembled on the field and warmed up, Coach Shiflet lined his young prospect up against each of his current team's backs, beginning with the youngest. One by one, Brooks passed each of the veteran football players, just as he had vanquished the young eighth grader a week earlier. Brooks ended his day's racing by convincingly defeating Rodney Cartmell. Rodney had starred on Junction's football team for four years, and he was graduating that spring. Soon, young Cartmell would be on his way to Waco to run the football for the Baylor Bears.

In the fifteen years Weldon Shiflet had been watching high school kids play sports, he had never seen anything approaching the performance Brooks Oakley put on that Friday afternoon. He could barely contain himself. But a life spent in the Hill Country had taught him to remain reserved. As Coach Shiflet walked past the stunned Cartmell boy, he extended his hand to Brooks. "I think you'll do, son," he said.

Junction was a small town. After lunch at home, Walter had driven to the courthouse on business. Everyone there was talking about Brooks. Walter arrived at the football field just in time to see Brooks race Rodney. He couldn't believe his eyes. But Walter remembered how proud he had been of Ralph, and how Ralph had pulled back when Walter had voiced his pride in his eldest son's athletic triumphs. Watching Brooks, Walter stood quietly—even though he wanted to jump into the air and shout out his excitement. "That was fine, Brooks," the father said, after Coach Shiflet had been the first to congratulate the young Oakley. Then Walter turned his attention to

Rodney. "You ran a great race, too, son," the judge told the vanquished athlete. "And I know the folks up in Waco will enjoy watching you play football every bit as much as we have here in Kimble County."

Walter drove Brooks home and was dying to rave about his son's performance. Even though the elder Oakley was bursting with fatherly pride, he only made one comment. "I'm very proud of you," he told his gifted young athlete. Fireworks were exploding inside Brooks' head. For three years, when he hadn't been working on the farm or studying, Brooks had concentrated on his dream. All the way home, he could see himself playing football on the lush grass in Austin, starring for the Texas Longhorns. Nothing could stop him now.

CHAPTER TWENTY-EIGHT

Brooks spent that summer working on his grandparents' farm in New Mexico with Luis Velasquez, Miguel's younger brother. Knowing that Brooks would begin playing football in the fall, Luis saw to it that Brooks pitched the most hay, dug nearly all the holes for fence posts, and did the heaviest work of anyone on the Little Hatchet. Each night after the work was done, Brooks spent his time talking with and reading to his grandmother. He did not remember James, his grandfather, who had died when Brooks was only three-years old. However, Rebecca, Brooks' grandmother, became a special person in his life. She talked with him for hours about what she dreamed for him, and she loved to hear her grandson read the Bible.

She had kept letters and some news clippings from when Ralph had played football in Tennessee, but she didn't really understand what football was. She did know that Ralph had been offered the opportunity to attend West Point but had passed up the chance. Each night that summer, before Brooks began reading the Bible for her, Rebecca urged Brooks not to miss the opportunity to receive an education at West Point or the Naval Academy. Brooks promised his grandmother that he would not repeat his older brother's mistake.

At least half-a-dozen times that summer, Rebecca also told her grandson about how his father had helped rescue Little Matt, Brooks' uncle and Walter's youngest brother, from the Mescalero. All of his older brothers and sisters had heard the story. But Brooks was the only one among his siblings who had truly appreciated what his father had done and understood how brave Walter had been. Fact was, Walter was too gentle, too jovial, too kind, and too outgoing for his family and neighbors to imagine how intensely courageous and determined Walter had been that summer in New Mexico so many years ago. Rebecca made sure that Brooks understood and would never forget what his father and grandfather had done to save Little Matt.

As soon as he returned to Telegraph, Brooks wrote a letter to the circulation manager of *The San Antonio Light*. He wanted to deliver their paper to the folks around Telegraph. He was willing to get up every morning, and make the deliveries for free, he told them. The circulation manager knew what Brooks did not—that the people who lived along the South Llano River could not afford a subscription to the newspaper. However, the newspaper man was so impressed by Brooks' determined offer that a copy of the paper was put on the train each night for the Junction High School library. In that way, Brooks got what he had wanted all along. He could read about the exploits of the University of Texas Longhorns playing football on Saturday afternoons in the fall. Each Monday morning from September through December, Brooks was waiting for Mrs. Apfel to open the library so he could read every word and statistic the paper printed about his heroes in Austin. The second week in November, there was something else in the *Light* for Brooks to read. Sam Potter of *The Junction Eagle* had mailed a story to San Antonio that the sports editor of the *Light* had picked up and played prominently. It was about the freshman running sensation of Hill Country football, Brooks Oakley of Junction High School. Mrs. Apfel allowed Brooks to cut the article out of the paper and take it home to his mother. Ada kept the clipping, beginning a scrapbook for Brooks in the same way she had saved Ralph's notices more than ten years before.

For most of the boys, practice was tedium. They liked the games they played after school on Fridays, but practice was boring, sweaty, hard work. Brooks loved every minute of his football experience, whether scrimmaging, hitting the tackling dummies, even running sprints. Because with each play, each hit, each lap, Brooks was one step closer to reaching his dream in Austin. Unlike the big cities, or the parts of the state where oil production and refining were booming, football in the Hill Country was primitive. There were no lights, meaning games were played in daylight. Most of the fields didn't provide seating of any kind. The students, players' families, and townspeople stood along the sidelines watching their young men. In Junction, as with most of the schools they played, the uniforms were makeshift. The pads and safety equipment were broken and mismatched. No player had a complete uniform. The jerseys weren't all the same color, and the shoes didn't fit. The best equipment went to the seniors; the next best to the juniors, and on down the list. Even though Brooks started every game that fall, he began wearing a uniform that was mostly rags. By November, Ada had repaired it so many times that more of the material in it was patch than original. Walter wanted to send to a sporting goods store in San Antonio for a decent helmet for Brooks. The leather on the one the school provided him was a tattered mess. There were holes in it and the left earflap had torn away, leaving that side of his face completely uncovered. The chinstrap had been tied to the left side of the helmet with three leather strips.

Afraid that it would shame the poorer boys on the team, Brooks pleaded with his father not to buy another helmet. Brooks also did everything in his power to keep the spotlight from shining too brightly on him. For someone so young, the rookie athlete had an uncanny appreciation that he was playing a team sport. Brooks had become the star of his team before the first half of his first game ended. But perceptively, Brooks knew that all the other boys on the team had to maintain a desire to play at the top limits of their ability if Brooks was to realize his dream of running for the Longhorns.

CHAPTER TWENTY-NINE

The Junction Eagles were small and inexperienced. The Fredericksburg Billy Goats were mostly seniors, and much larger. As for the archrival Kerrville Antlers, at the beginning of the season they appeared unstoppable. The young men from Kerrville outweighed the Junction players by nearly twenty pounds per man along the line. Three or four members of the Kerrville team seemed certain to play college football. Kerrville had even traveled all the way to San Antonio to play their first game of the season. The Antlers had held a much bigger school, Brackenridge High, to only seven points in San Antonio. The Antlers had barely missed tying the game in the closing seconds, when Brackenridge blocked an extra point just as time ran out.

If Junction were going to get the kind of attention Brooks needed it to have, everyone on the Eagles squad would have to play a lot better than most people thought possible. Brooks talked up his teammates day and night, telling them how good they were, congratulating them on every success, doing his best to make them feel confident in their ability. Coach Shiflet preached one message every practice. "If you know you're good, and you put in the work, you will be good," he told them. Every Friday afternoon, Junction continued to surprise opponents: Sonora, Brady, Mason—even Llano. It was the Monday after the Llano game that the *Light* had printed the feature story about Brooks. Junction was bursting with pride for their scrappy young football team. Everywhere the boys went, they were congratulated, patted on the back, and looked up to. That Friday after lunch as the school bus carrying the team left for Menard, the Eagles were cocky. They felt unbeatable.

The town of Menard was so poor their team couldn't afford real football shoes. In many Hill Country communities, children got one pair of shoes a year, at Christmas. Lots of children wore out or completely outgrew their shoes long before Christmas, and many kids came back to school in the fall barefoot. That was the way things were in Menard. As a result, in some years, many of the Menard players would have no shoes until Christmas. In such years, the whole team would practice and play in bare feet. So Coach Shiflet, as he had during other similar times, decided that the Junction team would voluntarily play without shoes against Menard. Coach Shiflet always wanted his team to exemplify good sportsmanship and fairness. But that virtuous gesture by Weldon Shiflet did not change an unfortunate fact. There was bad blood between the townspeople of Menard and Junction.

As soon as the Junction players stepped from the bus, it was clear that everyone in Menard had read or heard of the story about Brooks. The Menard players did not openly taunt Brooks, but they were pointing him out to each other. There were also memories of the near riot that had stopped the game two years earlier. The game had been delayed for almost two hours because Menard couldn't field enough players to make a complete team. The delay gave a large contingent from Junction time to drive to Menard. Finally two players who looked much older than the rest of the boys showed up, and the game began. After fighting broke out on the field several times, one of the men from Junction emerged from the dressing room in the Menard gymnasium. He carried two metal hard hats and two sets of coveralls stained with oil, sand, and mud—clearly the clothing of two men who had been working in the oil fields near San Angelo. This was conclusive proof to the fans from Junction that Menard had slipped two ringers into the game. An embarrassing brawl involving not only the players but also parents from both schools quickly ended the game. This was the background for the contest; and the fact that Menard had not won a game so far this season, increased the tension. In most of the games they had lost, the primarily freshman team fielded by Menard had not been able to keep the score close; but they were determined not to be embarrassed by Junction.

Menard took the opening kickoff for a touchdown. They stopped Junction from scoring in the first quarter and opened the second quarter with a time-consuming touchdown drive. Just before the half, Menard led by fourteen points. Junction rallied. Brooks ripped off four big gains in a row. With fifteen seconds remaining in the half, and the ball on the three-yard line, Brooks took a toss and ran a wide sweep around the right side of the Junction line. A skinny little kid with no shoulder pads and no helmet dived desperately at Brooks' ankles. Brooks flew into the air. He waved his left arm wildly trying to regain his balance. When a second Menard defender slammed into him, the ball popped out of the crook of his right arm. A third Menardsman grabbed the ball out of the air and raced ninety-eight yards for the third Menard touchdown. The mood was grim on the Junction sideline during half time. Usually, Coach Shiflet spent the intermission explaining what he wanted his team to do in the second half. However, that afternoon, Coach Shiflet stood without speaking, hoping the boys would recover from their overconfidence.

Brooks' team was stone faced as they took the field for the second half kickoff. The defense dug in, and Junction took control of the game on offense, scoring twice in the third quarter and twice early in the fourth. Then the Junction offense stalled, and the Panther defense hung on for dear life. Junction won twenty-eight to twenty-one. But when the game was over, the Eagles players were too tired to cheer. They climbed on board the bus, and most of the boys slept all the way home.

Monday, the young men were so exhausted and sore they could not practice. Tuesday, the Junction team stumbled onto the practice field to begin preparing to play Fredericksburg. Even with an extra day's rest, the Eagles were listless—even lifeless. By Wednesday, it seemed there was no hope. Watching his lethargic players, Coach Shiflet knew he had to do something. Ten minutes after he started the scrimmage, he blew his whistle loudly to stop the practice. "Everybody over here," he shouted. When his players were gathered, he began pointing as he spoke.

"I want the linemen over here, and the backs over there," the coach directed. "We're going to try something different. I want the backs on the line, and we'll rotate the linemen through the backfield." Coach Shiflet called a list of four names. Those four linemen would be the first to get an opportunity to run or pass the football. The coach huddled the offense, as the defense looked on apprehensively. Just as with the offense, Coach Shiflet had the boys who ordinarily played in the backfield up on the line. The bigger players were in the defensive backfield. Brooks was on the defensive line just as Bob McBride, the big defensive tackle, took the handoff from the other tackle, Charles Wilson. Brooks met Bob hard at the line of scrimmage. Eighteen yards later, Bob fell on top of Brooks who was still holding on for all he was worth. Everyone, even coach Shiflet, roared with laughter—everyone but Brooks.

Before Brooks had a chance to catch his breath, Charles smashed into him with the force of a freight train. This time, Brooks lost his grip on the big tackle after ten yards. Four of the other backs grabbed Charles, but no one could hold on, and Charles ran for a touchdown. Even Brooks was laughing now. Practice was fun for everyone. The players forgot how tired they were. They forgot their aches and pains and just had fun.

Coach Shiflet gave the team Thursday off to recover from the bruises and strains left over from Wednesday. When they boarded the bus after lunch on Friday, the Eagles were laughing and teasing. By the time the team arrived in Fredericksburg they were ready to play football, but so was Fredericksburg. The first half produced the same kind of futile defensive struggle Junction had seen in the fourth quarter the week before in Menard. There was no score. The third quarter was almost the same, but the strength and stamina of the bigger and faster boys from Fredericksburg seemed to be coming to the fore.

Just before the fourth quarter began, Neal Jones, Fredericksburg's fastest player, caught a pass directly in front of Brooks at the Junction sixteen-yard line. Brooks hit Neal with what he thought was a perfect shoestring tackle, but Neal stepped out of it and almost walked into the end zone. As Fredericksburg kicked off to begin the fourth quarter, Brooks stood determinedly at his own twenty-yard line. He took the ball running at full speed at his twenty-seven and dashed to the Fredericksburg twenty-nine. Brooks was all set to go on an offensive rampage, but Coach Shiflet signaled for a time out. He called his players to the side and realigned them, just as he had done during Wednesday's practice. The big guys were in the backfield and the backs were on the line. Brooks was horrified. He knew that the big linemen from Fredericksburg would run right over him on their way into Junction's backfield. He was right. They trampled him. However, by the time the tackle and guard who had run over Brooks reached Bob McBride, they were at full speed. Instead of tackling his ankles, the Fredericksburg linemen hit Bob upright. Brooks felt the Fredericksburg linemen a second time. This time they were falling on him from the opposite direction. Brooks had not seen it, because he was buried under Fredericksburg players. However when he regained his feet, Brooks watched Charles Wilson congratulating Bob, who had just scored a touchdown. Brooks tried to run to congratulate his teammate, but he was still woozy from the pounding he had taken and couldn't move. Bob McBride was beside himself with excitement.

It seemed to Neal Jones that Bob was on top of him before the Fredericksburg star caught the ball from the kickoff that followed Junction's touchdown. Neal was out cold for about three minutes, lying on his back at the Fredericksburg twelve-yard line. Finally the awful odor from the ammonia, which was being held up to his nose brought the Fredericksburg runner back to consciousness. On fourth down, Fredericksburg punted, but Robert Reinstrau fumbled on the Billy Goat two-yard line. The Fredericksburg drive stalled at the Junction forty-seven, and Fredericksburg was forced to punt. Brooks clinched his teeth as he took the high spiraling kick on his own one-yard line. He tore down the field like a person trying to outrun a bullet. All Brooks could see was the Fredericksburg goal line. Pursuing opposing players leaped desperately, hoping to tackle Brooks from behind. The pursuers were completely outside Brooks' field of vision as they fell painfully and futilely to the ground. Also behind Brooks' sight were the Junction players throwing blocks, which had stopped other Fredericksburg defenders before they could get close to Brooks. All the young Junction phenom could see clearly was the Fredericksburg end zone, where he stood alone after a run that fans in Junction would talk about for twenty-years. Junction won fourteen to seven.

When they arrived in Junction the following Friday, Kerrville's only loss was still the one-point defeat they had suffered in San Antonio to Brackenridge High School. Most of the people who lived in the town of Kerrville traveled to Junction to support their football team that Friday afternoon, and most of the population of Junction was waiting on the visitor side of the field. The game was no contest. Brooks scored eight touchdowns, two on kickoff returns. The final score was Junction fifty-six, Kerrville thirty-five. Brooks had ascended to the stratosphere of Texas high school football. He had become a legend.

CHAPTER THIRTY

Two brothers were never closer than Brooks and Ray. For the most part, their differences were complimentary. Certainly that was true in football. Ray, who now preferred to be called Amos, was the largest of the incoming freshmen at Junction High School despite being a year younger than most of his classmates. The first day of practice, only two members of the football team were larger, and they were both seniors. While anticipation and excitement had lifted spirits and expectations in Junction the previous year when Brooks had taken his place in the Eagles backfield, Ray's arrival passed with little notice.

Both brothers were competitive in the classroom, but with one difference. Brooks was deadly serious about his academic standing. Ray either did not care or perhaps pretended not to care. He was completely inattentive to his homework but made mostly A's anyway. Ray's teachers found his work habits frustrating. He remembered absolutely everything, which led to discussion among the teachers in Junction as to which Oakley brother was actually smarter. Ray's grades were nearly as good as Brooks'—leading the teachers to wonder what Ray might accomplish if he applied himself. Brooks overworked. He was endlessly curious about almost everything, but especially science and math. Ray was easy going to the point of appearing disinterested. Brooks wanted to attack every concept or problem, pick it apart, then put it back together. Brooks had even been known to be late for football practice, when a concept in geometry or biology was particularly troublesome to him. He simply would not leave the teacher alone until his curiosity was satisfied.

Ray hated football practice. It was boring and tedious. Of course, being a lineman accounted for some of Ray's problems. Above all, he hated the repetition of practice. Ray got everything the first time, always. That perspective erased the possibility in Ray's thinking that repetition would make him better. Ray felt he knew his job on the team. He was there to knock enough opposing players to the ground to create a lane for Brooks to scoot through for a big gain. Ray was excellent at knocking people down, so that aspect of his game didn't pose much of a challenge for him.

If Brooks had inherited Walter's meticulous nature, Ray had inherited his strength. However for Ray, that strength came with significantly more frame. He wasn't always the biggest player on the field, but he was always the strongest. Additionally, he was extremely quick —much quicker and more agile than most defensive lineman other teams lined up against him. For Brooks' first year, the team had to rely almost solely on the young runner's unbelievable speed to execute sweeps around opposing teams. When Ray came to play for the Eagles, there was always a big hole in the left side of the opponent's line that Brooks could run through. The easygoing younger Oakley brother saw to it.

At first Walter was worried that Ray would be disappointed because Brooks was a football star, and Ray was unlikely to become one. His father's concerns were unjustified. Ray was not at all jealous, but totally happy that Brooks got the glory. When he reached high school, things were no different for Ray than they had ever been. It had never occurred to him that he needed to be equal to Brooks. Ray never thought of himself as being inferior to his older brother. He just wanted to be with Brooks as much as he could. That's all he had ever needed from his brother, and high school didn't change that simple fact of Ray's life.

Ada's concerns for her youngest son were different. Every thought she had about Ray traced back to the countless hours she had spent nursing him, when he had been almost constantly sick as a baby and small child. Her memory was permanently scarred by the numerous instances when her frail son had nearly died. It had formed a pattern etched so deeply into Ada's mother memory that it had become indelible. Every time Ray coughed, his mother worried whether he was about to be taken away by a life-threatening illness. With Ray approaching six-feet tall and two-hundred pounds, Ada still thought of her youngest son as prone to sickness, a belief unsubstantiated by any current fact. Ray no longer became ill any more often than the other children.

His mother was also consumed by a deep concern that Ray might stumble onto the same path of destruction as his older brother Glenn had. Glenn, the family's wayward son, had been murdered three years before his thirtieth birthday. Ada had never thought of Glenn as mean, and certainly not as evil. She had only looked upon him as weak, too easily influenced by others. His mother knew that Ray was much brighter than his late older brother. But Ada was troubled by her observation that her youngest son was extremely likely to try almost any dangerous thing suggested to him. She was consumed by worry. Ada could not bear to have another child killed. She just would not permit something like that to happen twice. Several times a week, Ada took Brooks aside. "Keep Ray with you," she would instruct him. "Don't let him run off with boys who'll get him in trouble." Brooks always promised that he would be watchful. He never talked back to his mother or complained to her about the responsibilities she placed on him.

Not only was Brooks accepted as the family's leader among the seven living Oakley siblings by his mother, but by Walter and most of his older sisters as well. Only Ralph refused to embrace the role which Ada had decreed for the young Brooks. Ralph had hated Glenn because he was weak. He hated Brooks because he was a model son, a person his mother loved as much as she did Ralph. Because everyone in the family looked up to Brooks, Ralph's rightful place as oldest son could never have been realized. Ralph conveniently ignored the fact that he had run off to be a gangster, and how everyone else considered that to be a stain that the Oakley family could never be rid of. How unlikely it seemed that two such extraordinarily gifted sons could be in a single family.

Making matters worse, Ralph had never been comfortable with his father. Increasingly, Ralph drew away from the rest of his family because his little brother claimed the role of leadership to which Ralph, as eldest, believed was his absolute right. Ralph had been an unquestioned football hero; but he had done so far away and long ago, when most of the other children were too young to remember his heroics. Ralph could not so much as say hello to someone in Junction, or increasingly, even in San Antonio, without that person immediately launching into praise of Brooks as a football hero.

By the middle of his second season, everyone considered Brooks the most outstanding football player ever produced in the Hill Country. When they thought of Ralph at all, people remembered that he and his dead brother, Glenn, had been bootleggers. They might also recall that Ralph had been in jail for running illegal rum and whiskey. Ralph's previous football fame had faded, then disappeared. Ralph couldn't stand being thought of as inferior to Brooks, but Ray considered his oldest brother's discomfort hilarious. For most of his life, Ray had heard his parents and older sisters talk about Ralph as if he stood on the same plane with the ancient gods of Greece and Rome. Ray was greatly amused that Ralph, back home in Telegraph after a failed career in crime, was surrounded by the mountains of praise heaped on Brooks—the little brother Ralph despised. Ray had never liked Ralph because Ralph liked himself too much; because he was bossy; and because he had broken their mother's heart. Of course, Glenn had broken Ada's heart as well, but Ray had conveniently forgotten that sad fact. Ray had completely idolized Glenn. He remembered Glenn as the older brother who had taken time to play with Brooks and Ray. And he especially remembered the Christmas presents that Glenn had sent from Joske's every year. After Glenn's death, Christmas had never again been magical for Ray.

The third week of the football season, Ray skipped a practice to sneak off and smoke with some of his friends, the very friends that posed such a concern for Ada. Brooks never badgered Ray the way some big brothers do and seldom scolded him. However, the next morning before school without a word said, Brooks escorted Ray to Coach Shiflet's office in the gym. "Ray has promised me he won't miss practice again," Brooks told their coach. Of course, Ray had never had an opportunity to promise Brooks anything, since they had not spoken. "Is that true?" Coach Shiflet asked his big tackle. "Yes sir," Ray said firmly. "If you miss another practice, you're going to sit the bench for a week," Coach Shiflet said. "Do you understand?" Ray promised his beloved coach with a firm "Yes sir," and he kept the promise Brooks had made on his behalf. There were several days that fall that he skipped school, but Ray never missed another football practice.

Coach Shiflet, however, would not excuse Ray's absence from summer practice. As punishment, Ray sat on the bench for the Eagle's first game. Playing without Ray, Junction was lucky to beat San Marcos twelve to six. Brooks had an outstanding game. He scored both touchdowns and ran for two-hundred twenty-five yards. After Brooks' performance against San Marcos, not only were there writers from the San Antonio papers at the Eagles' game against San Angelo, but the *Dallas Morning News* and the *Houston Chronicle* sent reporters as well. This time, Ray was blocking for Brooks. Ray's nose was broken on the third play of the game, but Ray played until well into the fourth quarter when Junction's win seemed assured. When coach Shiflet pulled Brooks and Ray from the game, Brooks had scored three touchdowns, rushed for over three-hundred yards, and Ray had scored two points by forcing a safety against San Angelo. There was no doubt Brooks Oakley was going to be the leading rusher in Texas high school football history.

When Junction traveled to Fredericksburg for their third game of the season, Notre Dame asked a former tailback who was now a priest in Dallas to investigate this Texas running sensation. Father Kosnowski came into the locker room after the game to talk with Brooks and Coach Shiflet, and to offer Brooks a full scholarship to Notre Dame. Brooks was flattered. However, after listening to the priest tell wonderful stories about victories the Notre Dame Fighting Irish teams that he had played on had won, Brooks told Father Kosnowski that he was grateful for the offer. Then, standing and shaking the priest's hand, Brooks added, "Father, for as long as I can remember, the only place I have dreamed about playing football is the University of Texas. I'm not really sure how this scholarship business is done. I have to rely on Coach Shiflet for those things. Coach Littlefield came to watch, when we beat San Marcos on their field, earlier this year, so I'm pretty sure they want me. But even if the Longhorns don't give me a scholarship, I'm going to Austin and try out, even if I have to walk to get there."

"You have a great future ahead of you, Brooks," Father Kosnowski assured the young athlete, "and I'm sure the Longhorns will give you a scholarship and anything they legally can to get you to Austin. But if for any reason things don't work out for you there, Notre Dame wants you to play for the Irish. Coach Shiflet has my number, and you can call me collect anytime, even if you just want to talk or need some advice about what it takes to play college football. "Keep us in mind. We've got lots of wealthy alumni and supporters in Dallas who would love the opportunity to provide you and your parents with transportation to any one of our football games that wouldn't interfere with your games here in Junction, and you will be on the field right next to Coach Rockne. Of course, your parents would be the guests of President Walsh. You don't have to say anything. Just remember, it's an open offer.

"If you do wind up playing in Austin next year, I've already checked the schedule. The Longhorns will be playing Vanderbilt at the State Fair of Texas in Dallas on October 15, and you can bet I'll be there in the stands, cheering you on." The pair had a final handshake, and the priest clapped Brooks on the shoulder, just before Brooks excused himself to go celebrate with his teammates. As he walked away, Brooks laughed out loud. It was not a laugh at Father Kosnowski's expense. Brooks had been deeply moved by the priest's offer and astounded by the thought of standing on the sidelines next to Knute Rockne. The laugh had to do with Brooks' mother. The idea of Ada, who had grown up Methodist, and became a devout Presbyterian after her marriage to Walter, sitting at a football game in South Bend, Indiana, in the company of a Catholic priest was so far beyond his belief that Brooks just couldn't keep the unbelievability of such an event to himself.

Brooks had guessed correctly that President Walsh was almost certainly a priest, as well as being head of the university. And Brooks had known since his earliest childhood how deeply opposed to all things Catholic his mother was.

The Kerrville Antlers were given the best chance of spoiling Junction's undefeated season. The odds of that happening increased on the opening kickoff when Ray's right ankle was broken, ending his season. The contest remained scoreless until the final minute of the fourth quarter, when the Eagles gave the Antlers a shock by lining Brooks up at right tackle in place of Ludwig Mueller, the two-hundred-ten-pound replacement for Ray. The ball was on Junction's own twenty when Mueller, playing at tailback instead of on the offensive line, took the snap from center and ran for dear life around the right end. At first, the Kerrville linemen stood stunned, watching the big farm boy run. Three of the Antlers' defensive backs dived at Mueller's ankles. Two missed, and the third bounced harmlessly off Ludwig's rock-hard thigh. The Kerrville defensive tackle, who had been lined up opposing Brooks, had been sent sprawling by a lightning-speed, full-on block administered by Brooks. Initially, the dazed defender sat on the ground wondering what had happened to him as he watched with detachment while the big freshman for Junction ran. In a second or two, the downed defender regained his senses and pursued. Brooks saw the Kerrville tackle gaining on Ludwig and took off at top speed. Not only did he have to catch a fast player twenty yards ahead of him, but Brooks also had to get in front of the big tackle to avoid a clipping penalty.

The race ended on the Kerrville twenty-yard line. Brooks had leaped a split second before the Kerrville tackler made his move on Ludwig, and Brooks buried his right shoulder into the husky defender's abdomen. Ludwig's legs slipped easily out of the tackle's grasp, as the momentum from Brooks' block shoved the bigger man from Kerrville aside and sent the two rolling toward the sideline. Both players were nearly breathless, when Ludwig tripped on the six-yard line and fumbled the ball into the end zone. Back on his feet in an instant, Brooks landed on the ball just as the Kerrville defender crashed on top of Brooks and precisely as the starter's pistol popped to end the game.

Junction won six to nothing. Despite Ray's broken ankle and Brooks' four cracked ribs, Junction ended the season undefeated, and Brooks' name was written in the record book in Austin as the all-time leading rusher for a Texas high school football team.

At first, Ray stayed in bed with his cast, but when he got up the young man was clumsy on his crutches and impatient. Ten days after Doc Wimberly had put the plaster cast on his ankle, Ray slipped out to the barn and chipped it off with a hatchet. The result was predictable. Ray's ankle failed to heal properly.

Brooks devoted his spring to study. He wanted to be valedictorian of his class, but he was locked—as he had been since coming to Junction High School—in an academic tie with Mae Rosenfeld. Both had straight A's all through high school. So between themselves, they kept running totals of their numerical averages. As the final semester began, Brooks and Mae each had overall averages of ninety-eight-point seven percent. Starting that final spring, the two close friends and rivals computed their averages after each test. An advantage of five one-hundredths of a point on any given Monday after Friday tests sent the winner's spirits soaring. But the lead switched back and forth all term.

CHAPTER THIRTY-ONE

Brooks had a serious crush on Mae. He found her red hair and freckles beguiling. When they had taken trips as part of Junction High's debate team, the two spent as many hours together talking as they could manage. However, the Rosenfelds, who ran a small dry goods store, were staunchly religious, and they were the only Jewish family in the county. The Rosenfelds got along well with their neighbors, but they would never permit their daughter to be in any kind of social setting with a young man who was not of their faith. When Brooks invited Mae to be his date to the senior prom, her parents refused permission and would not discuss the matter with their daughter at all. Mae was broken-hearted and chose not to go to the prom. Brooks spent his prom night outside the gym in the company of all the other boys who did not have dates, where they sneaked whiskey and felt sorry for themselves. Traditionally, graduating students with at least B averages were exempt from final exams. Two weeks before finals, Brooks and Mae asked their teachers for permission to take the final exams to break the deadlock, but their requests were turned down. When the last tests before finals were graded, Brooks' and Mae's grades were still even. They would share the honor of valedictorian.

The weekend before graduation, several of Brooks' classmates who were exempt from finals organized what they called a senior trip to Padre Island. Brooks and two other boys borrowed cars from their parents. Fourteen boys, including some members of the football team who were not graduating, headed for the Gulf of Mexico, anticipating a great and memorable adventure. Ada was anxious about allowing Brooks to go on the trip, but Walter just laughed at her. Brooks had never been in any trouble of consequence in his whole life, and his father felt strongly that his sometimes too serious and much accomplished son deserved to have a grand time with his high school friends. If anyone had ever earned the right to celebrate, surely it was Brooks.

The boys left school early on Friday hoping to get onto the island before the ferry stopped running at nine p.m. They caught the last boat, which was packed with weekend beach goers. The boys from Junction reached the island and found a place to camp. Some of the boys brought canvas tarps that their fathers used to cover crops headed to market. The boys rigged the sections of the heavy cloth together with some tall oak poles they had cut at home. Working by lantern light, the young men erected their crude tent near the edge of the water. None of the Hill Country boys had ever been to the beach before.

As the sun's light first appeared on the horizon over the vast water, the boys quickly made a driftwood fire and cooked a hearty country breakfast, which they rapidly devoured. The young men were seventeen and eighteen years old, looking out at an exotic seascape totally different from what they had grown up with in the Texas hills west of San Antonio. Despite the hiccups that had arisen from their mislocated campsite, the excitement level for the Junction boys remained high and they were completely absorbed in a festive new adventure. An hour after the youngsters had laid their breakfast fire, the young men were splashing in the surf, having the time of their lives. None had bathing suits, so they swam in old school pants that their mothers had cut off and hemmed for the occasion. At first, the boys were self-conscious because they did not have store-bought swimwear. However as the morning wore on, the Kimble County boys observed that only a scant few of the other swimmers had them either.

The boys swam in the gulf all day, and by evening, the fair skinned young men from the Hill Country were all glowing with miserable sunburns. That evening, the boys felt lots of severe prickling as their cleaned and heavily starched dress clothes made war against their burned skins. But adventure was calling, overriding their sunburn pain. Six miles down the island stood an invitation to manhood—a giant outdoor beer hall. It bore the lofty title of pavilion and consisted of a huge plank floor laid on pilings about a foot above the sand. The whole structure was covered by a thatched roof suspended from telephone poles which had long ago been bleached white by the salt air and sun. Each summer the roof had to be replaced; and when hurricanes swept across the island, most of the planks had to be retrieved, and returned to their pre-storm location as well.

The pavilion was crude and trashy. But to the unsophisticated young men from Kimble County, it was an exotic nightclub, as grand as the places showcased in the late 1920s Saturday night radio broadcasts of live dance music played by orchestras conducted by famous men like Guy Lombardo and Paul Whiteman. The boys did suffer a serious and completely unexpected disappointment: there were no young ladies their age. In fact there were no girls at all, and only a few women—perhaps one for every twenty men or boys. As to appearance, none of the ladies at the Saturday evening soirée could be even charitably described as stunning. Had they been near home, the boys' mothers would never have allowed their sons to get anywhere close to any of the gentlewomen at the pavilion. The ladies drank Mexican beer and smoked cigarettes openly, and they shocked the boys from Junction by cursing as loudly and crudely as the sailors and laborers they had come with.

A polka band blared at an ear-splitting volume in the middle of the pavilion. The beer was cheap and plentiful. Before ten o'clock, several of the boys from Junction were sporting black eyes and split lips from fights. At least five of the fights had started after the high school boys had convinced one of the older ladies to dance with them. Brooks guzzled beer with the hardiest of his schoolmates. The truth was that Brooks had never had a drink of alcohol of any kind, until the night of his senior prom. Brooks managed to avoid fighting until midnight, when a donnybrook erupted. Eventually it involved all the Hill Country boys, local men, and most of the women in the pavilion. When the riot faded to an exhausted calm, the boys from the Hill Country retreated to their fathers' cars and headed back to camp.

CHAPTER THIRTY-TWO

Brooks' car was the last to leave. As soon as he drove clear of the noise of the pavilion, he was surrounded by the sounds of snoring drunken classmates. The other cars were about a mile ahead. When Brooks had driven halfway back to the camp, he inadvertently slipped his father's car into a soft spot in the sand. As he struggled to free the stuck Ford, rocking it back and forth by switching the transmission from first gear to reverse, and quickly repeating the process, he only succeeded in burying the car up to its axles in the loose sand near the dunes.

Brooks roused his sleeping friends, who were ill from drinking too much beer. The boys worked as hard as they could. They lifted and shoved until several of them threw up, but the car could not be coaxed out of the sand with only their muscles. Brooks rallied his wits through the haze that had come from drinking too much beer. There were no shovels to dig the car out, so the boys used their hands. When they had dug as much sand away as they could, Brooks lined the boys up along the outline of the car to push while he worked the gears and clutch as rapidly as he could. The gears ground, and the clutch and tires smoked. The boys strained and rocked and fell. The car lurched forward, but only the front wheels came free. The back wheels were quickly buried in the sand, up to the rear-end housing.

The boys dug some more, but Brooks looked things over and decided that digging alone was not enough. He devised a strategy to raise the rear end of the car out of the sand with the jack. He planned to set the wheels in motion as the boys pushed the car off the jack. At first, the jack just sank in the sand, but Brooks found some driftwood to spread the weight and keep the base of the jack from boring into the sand as the jack was operated. Several attempts to raise the car failed. Each time it was elevated, the Ford wobbled and fell off the jack.

Finally, Brooks got the rear of the car as high out of the sand as the jack would permit. While he worked with the jack, the rest of the boys tried to clear a path for the rear wheels, digging with their hands. Brooks called them to the rear of the car and positioned them to push. Just as he started selecting points for the boys to push, Brooks spotted some obstructing sand directly under the housing for the differential and kicked at it with his left leg, which was fully extended beneath the car. At the same time, Albert, the biggest of the boys, heaved and began to vomit. As Albert bent to throw up, he lost his balance and fell backward into the jack. The Ford dropped into the sand with the differential housing landing solidly on Brooks' left ankle and shin. Brooks cried out in pain as his bones splintered. Hearing Brooks scream, the boys grabbed the rear of the car and lifted it off Brooks' leg. While they had the Ford elevated, they shoved it forward with all their collective strength, moving the vehicle onto firm sand. As soon as his leg was freed from the weight of the car, Brooks lost consciousness. With the car settled on firm wet sand, Brooks' friends carefully lifted him and carried him to the front of the car where they could examine his leg in the illumination of the headlights. His teammates gasped at the sight of Brooks' mangled and bloody leg. Each of them was immediately certain Brooks would never run on a football field again.

The boys quickly drove Brooks to the ferry landing, but the boat had stopped running hours earlier. Albert swam across the mile-wide lagoon, but there was no one on or near the boat. He had to run almost two miles in his bare feet to a coin telephone. An operator contacted the sheriff's office, and twenty minutes later a deputy in a patrol car towing a small trailer with a rowboat showed up. An ambulance followed, and Brooks was soon transported to a hospital in Corpus Christi. Sheriff Givens arrived at the emergency room about five minutes after Brooks and learned the name of the injured boy from his deputy. There was still no phone on the Oakley farm, so Sheriff Givens called Sheriff Wilson. Before leaving for the farm to get Walter, Sheriff Wilson phoned Doc Wimberly. Doctor Wimberly immediately called the hospital in Corpus Christi. After the nurse had described the injury to him, Doctor Wimberly placed a call to the University of Texas Medical Branch in Galveston and requested that a specialist from the medical school meet him in Corpus Christi. Sheriff Wilson, Doc Wimberly, and Walter drove all night, arriving at the hospital around eight in the morning. The doctor from Galveston reported two hours later, and Brooks was taken immediately to surgery. The specialist from the University of Texas, a local surgeon, and Doctor Wimberly worked on Brooks until four in the afternoon.

By the time the multiple operations were finished, Ray had driven Ada from Telegraph to the Corpus Christi hospital. Ada and her youngest son joined all the Kimble County boys on the senior trip. They had gathered to wait for news about their friend and legendary teammate. Doctor Wimberly was exhausted as he spoke with Ada and Walter in the hall. "Brooks is going to be okay," he told them. "He'll keep the leg, but I'll be amazed if he ever walks again without assistance." Ada screamed, and Walter and Doctor Wimberly both moved to comfort her.

"It's all right, Ada," the doctor consoled. "I think Brooks will be able to get around, but it looks like he's going to need a crutch or a cane." Ada bit her bottom lip to stop crying.

Friday night, Brooks was back in Junction for graduation. The doctors had put Brooks' leg in a cast all the way to his hip to keep his leg immobile. Brooks sat on the stage in a wheelchair, but he hobbled to the podium using crutches. With one crutch under his left arm, he firmly gripped the dais with his right hand as he and Mae jointly delivered the valedictory message they had written together.

Brooks spent his entire summer making the long and grueling drive between the University of Texas hospital in Galveston and a hot springs resort near Llano. No resource of the University of Texas went untapped. The day football practice began in Austin, Brooks sat in the doctor's office in Galveston with his father. For two weeks, Brooks had been able to limp along without a cane, but the movement in his ankle was so slight that it was barely noticeable. "I'm afraid that's the best we are going to be able to do, Brooks. It's a miracle that you can walk without a cane, but you're not going to run again. The injury was just too severe," the doctor explained, trying his best to conceal his disappointment. The doctors' collective best had just not been enough.

"I understand that I won't be able to play this year," Brooks said, forcing back tears. "But what if we spend the rest of the year with more therapy? What about next year?"

The doctor looked at the young football player, unable to conceal his disappointment. "Believe me Brooks, no one wanted to see you on that football field in Austin more than me, but it's not going to work. No matter how much physical therapy you go through, the ankle just won't move enough for you to run."

There was a long silence as Brooks let the news sink in. Finally the doctor resumed the discussion. "What did you want to do after football?" he asked.

"Well, I had never thought of anything other than football, until I came here the first time," Brooks sighed. "But since then, I've had a lot of time to think, and I believe I want to be a doctor."

The surgeon placed a hand on Brooks' arm. "With your grades and obvious intelligence, I don't doubt that you will make an excellent physician," the doctor predicted. "Things work out for the best. I'll leave you and your father alone here for a while, so you can talk," he added as Walter rose to his feet.

"Doc, we're abundantly grateful for everything you've done for Brooks. We can never thank you enough," he announced.

"Think nothing of it, judge," the surgeon responded, stepping toward the door.

"But Doc, no one's ever said a thing about money," Walter posed.

"And no one will, Judge Oakley. This one was on the alumni association and the University of Texas Medical Branch. Brooks was the most promising football player we have had in our lifetimes. And we decided the first day that if there was any way on God's earth, any chance under any circumstances, Brooks Oakley was going to play for the Longhorns, we were determined to make that happen. We did everything we knew. We did our absolute best. But we just couldn't make it work out," he concluded sadly.

The door clunked shut behind the departing doctor, leaving Brooks and Walter sitting in silence for more than five minutes. "I know playing football in Austin has been your dream for most of your life," Brooks' father began finally. "And while that was possible, your mother and I would never have done anything to interfere. But earlier in the summer, when it seemed like your football days were finished, I felt I should make some calls. Senator Sheppard promised me that, if you can pass the physical next spring, he will see to it that you get an appointment to West Point. Meantime, he suggests you spend a year at A&M boning up on your math. "You know," Walter continued, his voice cracking, "I always wanted to be an engineer, and my father always wanted me to be one. Maybe it's time we finally got an engineer in the family."

Brooks thought back to the promise he had made to his grandmother years before. He had told her that if he had the opportunity to attend West Point, he wouldn't pass it up the way Ralph had. Brooks recounted the promise for his father. "You know, Papa," Brooks continued, struggling to control his emotions, "I would do almost anything to make you and Momma happy. I think you deserve it, but I really want to be a doctor. I hate to say this after I've disappointed you the way I did, but being an engineer just doesn't interest me, and I want even less to be a soldier. I know this is something you've thought through, but I just never wanted to go to A&M. The only place I ever wanted to go to school was the University of Texas, and that's the only place I want to go, now," Brooks concluded. The young man studied his father's face. Walter was getting old, but he looked ancient that afternoon in Galveston. Walter couldn't hide his disappointment, but he tried his best.

"Well," he said, nearly crying, "we'll stop off in Austin on the way home, and see about the arrangements."

Realizing that the strain on Ada caused by Brooks' ordeal was almost more than she could endure, Ray successfully fought a daily battle against what he called his restlessness all summer. However, on the day after Brooks and Walter returned to Telegraph, Ray caught a freight train for Chicago.

CHAPTER THIRTY-THREE

In Austin, Brooks quickly became independent, taking a job in a cafe on Congress Avenue to pay his way through the university. He wrote his parents that the lady who owned it had provided a room above the restaurant for Brooks to live in, and he returned all the cash his father had given him for school, mailing his father a money order for the full amount. Brooks knew he was not doing what Walter wanted for him, and he didn't like knowing that his father was paying money to a school he seriously opposed. Walter sent the money order back to his son several times. But each time, Brooks returned it folded in with a letter home.

Brooks left campus every day in time to be at the restaurant to work lunch. Each evening, he was back at his post in the restaurant to assist with dinner and sometimes was on duty all night. The Longhorn was the only restaurant in Austin that stayed open twenty-four hours. Because they never closed, at least once a week someone failed to show up for work—even with the Depression on, and jobs nearly impossible to find. Brooks always filled in for the absent employee. He went to class, studied and worked. That was his routine, and the routine became his life.

The players on the U.T. football team regularly ate in the restaurant, chatting with Brooks and treating him as a teammate. Occasionally one would remark "hope you're with us next year," but no one ever mentioned Brooks' injury. Usually, Brooks walked the twelve blocks from the campus to the restaurant. He only took the streetcar when it was raining or when he was in an exceptional hurry. The more he walked, the stronger his ankle became. At least, that's the way it seemed to Brooks. By November, he only displayed the slightest trace of a limp.

Brooks attempted running for the first time in December. His effort produced forward motion which seemed more of a trot than a run. His ankle hurt for two days after, but Brooks forced himself to keep walking to build up strength in his nearly destroyed ankle and leg. The second time he ran, Brooks moved slightly faster, and his pain was less intense. Brooks hoped his ankle would be strong enough for spring football practice, but he never told anyone that he had begun running. Two weekends before practice started, Brooks went to the intramural field where some men were playing softball. When their game ended, Brooks spoke with one of the players and asked him to run against him for a hundred yards. It was the first time in his memory that Brooks had been beaten in a footrace. The other young man finished ten yards ahead of Brooks.

"Are you a fast runner?" Brooks asked the young man, after he had caught his breath.

"No, not at all. I just enjoy playing baseball. Why did you want to race me?" the young man wondered.

"I got hurt last year," Brooks explained. "I've been getting faster, but I had to run against someone to see how well I was doing."

The young man looked into Brooks' eyes. "So, how did you do?" he asked.

"Not very well, I'm afraid," Brooks conceded. "But thanks for running with me."

Just after the Fourth of July, Brooks took the train to Galveston. He told the doctor what he had been doing and asked him to examine his ankle. "Slip your pants off," the doctor instructed. He measured both Brooks' legs carefully in several places. After he recorded all the measurements on a chart, he wrote a note on a prescription pad. "Take this down to X-ray," the doctor instructed. About two hours later, the doctor called Brooks back into his office. "Here, these are the X-rays taken today," he resumed. "And these are the ones we took last summer. Now look over here," the doctor directed, pointing to the x-ray of Brooks' right ankle. See all these dark spots? They're cartilage. They're what allows your foot to move. Now look back at today's X-rays of your left foot, and tell me where the cartilage is," the doctor said to Brooks.

"I can't," Brooks answered after studying the pictures carefully.

"Why can't you?" the doctor asked.

"I don't know why. I just don't see any dark spots," Brooks replied.

"That's because your bones are fused together. The best I could do for you was put everything back in place, and let the bones grow together," the doctor explained.

"Roll up both your pant legs to your knees and circle your fingers around each calf right above the ankle," the doctor instructed Brooks. "What do you notice?" he continued.

"The left leg is much bigger," Brooks answered.

"That's right," the doctor confirmed. "You have completely distorted the muscles in your left leg, all the way up to your hip. And I would guess you've dramatically changed the muscle structure in your lower back as well. That's why you can run."

Brooks was encouraged. "So if I keep working, will I get enough speed back to play football?" Brooks asked.

"No son," the doctor sadly corrected his patient's mistaken conclusion. "I can't believe you've gotten this far without seriously injuring your back muscles. But if you keep doing this, even if you don't hurt your back, you'll break your ankle again. You'll probably do it just running. And if you were to try playing football, one good hit to your lower legs, and the ankle will snap. You have no flexibility in that ankle. Those fused bones can't move, or absorb shocks, so they will break."

CHAPTER THIRTY-FOUR

Brooks was devastated by the news. He rode the train back to Austin. For several weeks, Brooks couldn't bear to tell anyone what he had learned in Galveston. Finally, having to let the hurt out, he wrote to Mae, telling her of all his hard months of training, and explaining what the doctor had told him in Galveston. Mae wrote back to Brooks. And in September on her way back to Texas Woman's College in Denton, she left her train in Austin and walked up Congress Avenue to see Brooks at the Longhorn.

"We can't talk here," Brooks told her immediately, when Mae sat down at the counter. In less than a minute, Brooks made his arrangements and whisked Mae out the door. She was stunned, and Brooks felt stares on his back as the two bolted onto the sidewalk along Congress Avenue.

"I thought you'd be glad to see me," Mae declared, bewildered by the reception she had received. Brooks led her half a block down the avenue, then turned right, crossed the street and walked her up the hill to the west. They were going so fast that Mae was almost trotting to keep up. A block away from Congress Avenue, Mae jerked to a halt and pulled Brooks' elbow toward her. "If I'd known you were going to be embarrassed by my visit, I wouldn't have risked being late getting back to school," she told Brooks, her eyes burning directly into his. Mae was not going to wait any longer for Brooks to explain his shocking treatment of her. Still Brooks didn't say anything, and Mae pondered whether she could make a run back to the train before it pulled out of the station. She was humiliated. Mae had looked back toward the railroad station. When she turned to face Brooks again, Mae discovered an emotion she had never imagined she would see from her friend—fear. Brooks' eyebrows were arched, causing the skin on his forehead to wrinkle. He was troubled, apprehensive, and unquestionably afraid. Additionally, she noticed for the first time that Brooks had begun to lose his hair.

Maybe this wasn't the right time to leave, Mae thought. Brooks probably did need to talk to her, but just didn't know how to explain the things that were troubling him. Silently, and at a more reasonable pace, Mae walked with Brooks to the little square south of the courthouse. The park sloped down from all four sides and a picturesque white covered bandstand stood in the middle. Brooks led Mae down the hill to the bandstand and they sat down on its steps.

"Do they have concerts here?" Mae asked after a long silence.

"Yes," Brooks replied.

"And do you ever come?" Mae asked, not wanting to allow the silence to descend on them again.

"No," Brooks answered.

"I thought when I got your letter that you needed someone to talk to," Mae said, still trying to draw her friend into conversation. Brooks made no reply. "You know Brooks, I do realize that I'm the only friend you have in this situation," Mae chided. "I completely understand that you can't talk to any of your big football hero buddies about the permanence of your leg injury," she added, returning her eyes so she was looking directly into Brooks' eyes. At that point, Mae realized that her friend appeared to be close to tears.

"Thanks for coming," he managed at last. "I'm just not sure I can talk to you. I think I said everything I had to say in the letter. I guess I just needed someone to listen." Mae's face softened. She had gotten over the initial shock of what she had taken as rejection by Brooks.

"And I'm not sure you can carry around so much disappointment by yourself," Mae responded.

"I don't know what else to do about all this," Brooks said. "It's my burden, and I don't think anyone else can or should shoulder it for me," he offered.

"You feel sorry for yourself, don't you?" Mae suggested.

"Yes," admitted the former high school star.

"Because you can't play football at the university?" she continued.

"It was my dream, and now it won't happen," Brooks answered.

"But now you have a new dream. You want to be a doctor, don't you?" Mae queried.

"I do, but it's not the same," Brooks asserted.

"Why? Because it's not big enough? Because it's a sissy dream? Or because it's not a little boy's dream, like playing football, and listening to people yell for you, and scream out their adulation?" Mae probed.

At that point Brooks realized why he had written to Mae—because she was the most honest person he knew, and because she understood him better than anyone except for his mother. Brooks began feeling better about things, but Mae continued speaking. "Well I have a dream, too," she was telling him. "I want to be a doctor, just like you do. I'm just as smart as you, but why don't you ask your doctor friend down in Galveston how many women they admitted to the medical branch this fall? Was it any at all? Or was it perhaps one or two? Do you think I'm the second smartest woman in college in Texas, Brooks? Do you think I'm going to get in?" she demanded.

"No, I don't think you're the second smartest woman in college in Texas. I don't even think you're the smartest woman in college in Texas," he answered. Now it was Mae who appeared on the verge of crying. "I think you're the smartest woman in Texas, period," Brooks proclaimed. Brooks and Mae burst into laughter, and Mae wrapped her arms around Brooks' neck hugging him tightly.

"I hope you're right," Mae said.

They sat in the park talking, speaking no more of Brooks' problems. They talked about their dreams, and what becoming doctors would be like. A lot of the conversation was about all the competition they had enjoyed through school and the good times they'd had traveling with the debate team. When the sun was about to set, Brooks and Mae walked back to Congress Avenue, caught the streetcar and rode it across the river to the Nighthawk. Brooks ordered dinner for Mae but did not get anything for himself. He explained that he usually waited until midnight for his late meal.

"I'll pay for my own supper, if you want to eat," Mae offered.

"No, that's really not it, the money I mean. I just don't get hungry until midnight," he explained. Just before nine, a man a few years older than Brooks and Mae came up to their table. "Mae," Brooks began as he rose to his feet. "I'd like you to meet Harry Aiken. He owns the Nighthawk."

Harry had a wonderful smile and a kind face. "It's nice to meet you, Mae," Harry said. "I'm glad Brooks brought you down to this end of the avenue for a good meal." Everyone laughed. Harry asked Mae some questions about where she was from, her family, why she was in Austin, and when she was returning to school? It was all pleasant conversation. Then Harry became serious.

"You know Mae, you're the first girl I've ever seen Brooks with. Brooks has been in Austin for a year. And for most of that time, I've been trying to talk him into coming to work for me. I've even offered to make him a partner, but he won't listen. Do you think you can talk some sense into him?" Mae smiled.

"Brooks wants to be a doctor, Harry," Mae answered. "I know," Harry responded. "But that's way off in time. Brooks could be making the kind of money doctors make right now, if he would listen to me."

"It's not the money," Mae said, as if she were answering for Brooks. Harry feigned exasperation.

"Well, I can see it's no use talking to you either. Just the same, I'm really glad to see you, and I hope you'll stop by and visit often. Whenever you do, just like tonight, the meal is on me," Harry announced, displaying another broad smile.

"You can't make a million dollars giving food away," Brooks teased. "Of course, maybe giving this food away is the only way you can get rid of it." Everyone laughed. Brooks tried to pay, but Harry refused and told his cashier not to take the money. Brooks left a tip, and he and Mae walked up Congress Avenue to the Katy passenger station. The ten o'clock train for Dallas was thirty minutes behind schedule, so Mae just barely made it.

Mae was late for registration the next morning and spent thirty minutes begging the dean not to write to her parents. She stayed up most of that night penning a long letter to Brooks, telling him how much she loved him. It was nearly ten days before she received a letter back from Brooks.

"I love you, too," he wrote. "But I'm not sure what that means for us. It's a long way until the end of medical school. "I doubt you'll still want me by the time we're finished," he concluded. Mae wrote Brooks every night, and Brooks wrote back about once a week. Many of their letters were fiery and passionate. Some were thoughtful, and a good number were argumentative. The Christmas break came, and Mae looked forward to seeing Brooks in Junction, but he stayed in Austin. He had to work, he said.

Mae wanted to stop in Austin desperately as her train passed through in January, but she had promised herself she would not chase Brooks. Hard as it was, she kept her resolve. And the tone of the letter she wrote when she reached Denton was almost angry.

"You could have come home, if you had wanted," she wrote. Brooks did not answer right away. But when he finally did, his letter was somewhat rambling. Near the bottom of his letter, Brooks admitted that he was training again for a last try at football. Mae thought Brooks was being foolish. But uncharacteristically, she kept her doubts out of her letters. Brooks' correspondence became increasingly distant and preoccupied. He didn't mention his running, but Mae felt she could read it in Brooks' handwriting.

In April, Mae's family began making arrangements for their daughter's future. Mae was formally introduced to Dr. Josef Lebowitz and his family. Dr. Lebowitz had recently begun his medical practice in Dallas, where his family had a department store that catered to the city's lower income white population. In December, Mae and Josef were engaged. In June of the following year, they were to be married.

CHAPTER THIRTY-FIVE

When Brooks started running again, he realized he wasn't going to play football. So he asked himself why he was training. For Mae, Brooks represented a gamble of everything she had. It seemed all but certain to her that her family would be alienated forever if she were to become seriously involved with him. For Brooks, Mae was a risk. He loved her. In fact, he was certain that he could never love any other woman as much. However in Brooks' calculation, Mae required more of himself than he was willing to give up to anyone. If their involvement grew too fast, Brooks might not become a doctor. He might be in the restaurant business forever. Having lost football, Brooks would not gamble with the only big dream he had left. Brooks felt Mae was pushing him too far, too fast—demanding a level of commitment he was not prepared to give.

So Brooks pretended to be making a final try at football. It took all his spare time, even most of his letter writing time. When Mae wrote about meeting Josef, and her fear that her parents were attempting to arrange a marriage, Brooks felt cornered. He quit writing altogether. Even when Brooks accepted that his injury had shattered his football dreams, he had remained sure of his judgment. However, when Mae traveled to Austin a month after her engagement to explain what was happening to her life, how it was spinning away from her control, Brooks fell into confusion. Mae implored Brooks to give her some sign that he was serious about a future for the two of them. Brooks confessed he was unsure, and he did not offer the commitment the love of his life was begging him for. In tears, Mae boarded the train back to Denton six hours earlier than she had originally scheduled.

With her wedding a month away, Mae wrote Brooks a final letter. "Do you love me?" she pleaded to know. "If you say yes, I'll call this marriage off. I don't want to marry Josef, but I won't be able to stand the certain loss of my family if you won't have me."

Brooks wrote back: "I do love you, but I'm not sure I will ever get married." What was he talking about? Brooks wanted to race the letter to Denton and steal it from Mae's mailbox before she could read it. Of course he wanted her, but he could not lie. Brooks had really convinced himself that he might never marry. In fact, he was sure he would never marry if he did not marry Mae. No one else could possibly compare with her. If he was going to risk ruining his own life by not committing, he would not take Mae down with him. He let the letter, and Mae's marriage to Josef go without protest.

The week before Christmas, Brooks received a letter from Mae telling him what a terrible mistake the marriage had been. Josef would never permit her to go to medical school. He was ready to have children. Her dreams were destroyed, her heart was broken, and she hated herself for letting Brooks, her true love, get away. Brooks almost ran to the train station. In less than seven hours, he stood knocking on her door.

"I shouldn't have written," Mae spoke in a distant monotone when she saw Brooks standing on the porch.

"Then, you're not unhappy?" Brooks asked.

"Oh, I am," Mae conceded, tears filling her eyes. "I am far more unhappy than I told you in the letter. Josef is colder than snow. He makes me cry, and he makes me sick, and he doesn't even care. He's an awful man who doesn't believe people should be in love. He has never been happy, and he doesn't want anyone else to be happy, either. But I can't ask you to get me out of what I should never have gotten myself into."

Brooks said nothing. He simply walked past Mae and took a seat on her sofa. An hour later, when Josef arrived, Brooks was still sitting in the same place. Before Josef could close the door, Brooks had pounded his fist into the doctor's chin with lightning speed, knocking Josef through the open doorway, off the porch and onto his front yard. When Josef came through his door a second time, Brooks shoved Mae's letter into his face. Josef read it carefully. His face was bruised from Brooks' blow, but Josef showed no expression. Mae had watched from a hallway off the living room. Josef walked past Brooks, past Mae, and into a bedroom in the back of the house. When he returned to the living room, Josef pointed a .25 caliber pistol straight at Brooks' nose. As Josef spoke for the first time, Brooks noticed a trace of a Polish accent.

"I am not the athlete you are, Mr. Oakley, so I have no intent of being assaulted by you again. My wife may stay or go with you. That's her choice, but you must leave at once," Josef pronounced in a tone that was distant, cold, and absolutely serious.

Brooks looked at Mae. She did not move. He looked past the gun into Josef's face. Josef was still intensely focused on Brooks, and Josef's hand seemed to hold the small pistol skillfully. Brooks backed out the door and closed it behind him. He stepped to the side but waited on the porch expecting to hear gunfire. Brooks waited for more than three minutes without hearing any shots. He backed off the porch, and up the sidewalk to the street. Brooks waited again. Hearing nothing, he turned and walked to the streetcar. When the car stopped, he stepped on and rode toward downtown.

Brooks found a drug store and walked to the counter in the back. He told the pharmacist he had a diagnosed sleeping disorder but had left his prescription at home. He handed the druggist a ten-dollar bill and the druggist handed Brooks two pint bottles of Canadian whiskey in a white paper sack.

"Bring your prescription with you the next time you come in," the man behind the counter said, keeping all of Brooks' money.

Brooks walked out the door and back onto McKinney Avenue feeling like a wino. He pulled the cork from one of the bottles and swallowed half of it at once. Brooks started to put the cork back in the half empty bottle but reconsidered. He winced from the burn the alcohol had made in his throat, took a deep breath, and downed the rest of the bottle. Brooks was fuming inside, and hoped the whiskey would calm him. The dominant picture in his mind was Mae standing in the hall. Why had she written to him in such desperate anguish and pain if she didn't intend to leave? The other image was of the gun in his face. Irrationally, Brooks did not consider what he had done an invasion of Josef's home. Brooks was fixated on an unacceptable fact. He had let another man hold a gun on him and done nothing about it. Brooks, who had never seen a person point a gun at another, was enraged. He should not have let Josef leave the room to get the gun. Brooks should have taken the gun from Josef and beaten the doctor senseless. Brooks Oakley was not the sort of man one pointed a gun at.

As the whiskey took hold, Brooks wondered with whom he was angrier—Mae for staying or Josef for threatening Brooks with the gun? The argument orbited through his mind. Brooks drank the second bottle of whiskey as he had the first, then went to another pharmacy and bought two more bottles. This time, the whiskey in the bag came from Ireland. It didn't matter. Brooks had no taste for liquor. The next morning, Brooks woke, his head in a fog from the whiskey. To make Brooks' gloom complete, he was surrounded by an actual fog in the air. He sat against a wall between two buildings across the street from Josef's office. Brooks watched for an hour before Josef walked into his medical office. Brooks kept his eye on the door, as he walked halfway down the block to a bakery where he bought some rolls. Brooks ate half the bread, then fell asleep. Around two in the afternoon, Brooks woke again with a splitting headache. He found another drug store, ordered a coke at the soda fountain counter, but drank four glasses of water instead, and returned to the spot where he had been keeping vigil. Brooks ate the rest of the bread, took several pulls from his last bottle of liquor, and felt better.

When Josef came out of his office late in the afternoon, Brooks followed his streetcar for two blocks on foot until he could climb on and sit at the back of the car away from the doctor. Josef got off the car at Union Station. Brooks continued riding the streetcar across the Trinity River, jumped off in Oak Cliff, and raced back across the bridge on foot to find Josef boarding a train for Kansas City. Brooks thought for a minute, then walked to a pawn shop on Commerce Street. For five dollars, he bought a .38 caliber pistol, then went into the alley to drink what was left of his whiskey. Brooks found a drug store to replenish his supply of liquor. Still reeling from the alcohol he had just inhaled, Brooks drank half of one of the bottles he had just purchased and headed back to the depot.

"I want a ticket on that train," Brooks told the agent.

"Where to, son?" the elderly man asked him.

"Oklahoma," Brooks replied, spilling out the only word that came into his mind.

"Could you narrow that down for me? Ardmore, Pauls Valley, Norman ... "

Brooks interrupted with a single word, "Ardmore." He shoved a five-dollar bill underneath the bars.

"Two seventy-five," the agent said. Brooks reached in for his ticket and change. He felt the gun in one pocket, and whiskey in the other, as he moved toward the train. Brooks walked through the train several times, searching for Josef. A few miles north of Denton, Brooks saw Josef seated in the dining car. It was almost an hour before Josef finished his meal and encountered Brooks in the vestibule between train cars. Brooks was breathing heavily, and he reeked of whiskey. Josef felt the gun touch his head just in front of his ear before he saw Brooks.

"I don't think you want to throw your life away by killing me, Mr. Oakley," Josef said.

"You put a gun in my face," Brooks said determinedly.

"It was the only defense I had," Josef responded. "Mae and I have a bad marriage. If I had let you beat me anymore, I could have never faced her again." After a long pause, Josef concluded that it was unlikely Brooks was going to shoot him. It was far less certain to Brooks, who had no interest in this conversation. "Think for a moment, Mr. Oakley," Josef urged. "Mae asked you to set her free from a bad marriage. You did what she asked, but she did not leave the marriage. Surely, there must be a message there."

The alcohol clouded Brooks' wits, but Josef's words sounded reasonable—even through Brooks' alcohol fueled stupor.

"Why didn't she leave you?" Brooks challenged.

"It's our culture. She cannot," Josef responded.

"But Jews believe in divorce," Brooks shot back, uncertain where he might have gotten that piece of information.

"Mae could easily divorce me, but she cannot divorce her parents, or her heritage. Even though she spent her life among gentiles, Mae is a Jew, and she wants to go on being a Jew. I also think she knows you don't want to marry her. You only came to rescue a friend in trouble." Josef said. He paused to measure how well he was doing in his attempt to reason with Brooks. "That is right, isn't it Mr. Oakley?" he asked.

How could Josef know? Brooks tried to construct how Josef had pieced this narrative together, and how close to true it might be. All the while Brooks' brain fought against the alcohol, which was inhibiting his ability to reason. Brooks felt his finger on the trigger. If he were to kill this man, now was the time. Brooks' rage was melting to Josef's logic.

"I think it is. But how do you know?" Brooks said.

"Mae," Josef answered. "We talked after you left. She told me she wanted to go with you when you left but couldn't. She said she was afraid you only came because you felt sorry for her."

Brooks was almost through—ready to be done with this whole business. But he had one more question. "Why won't you let her go to medical school?" he asked.

"I'm jealous," Josef admitted. "You'll be there for one thing. I doubt I could ever win her back from medicine once she starts her studies. But getting her back from medicine and you—I could never do that." Brooks immediately objected as a lawyer might in a courtroom.

"You have money, Dr. Lebowitz," Brooks stated, letting the pistol in his hand drop down to his side. "You could afford to send Mae to school somewhere other than Galveston," Brooks said, intending his words as a challenge but realizing that they sounded more like a suggestion.

"You're right, Mr. Oakley. I could, and perhaps I will. Maybe I will find enough courage to do just that," Josef said, seeming to acknowledge the merit of Brooks' proposal. Brooks hurled the gun through the open window of the vestibule, and Josef exhaled. Seconds later, Brooks threw the rest of his whiskey out the same window. The train had been slowing for several minutes. Before it could come to a complete stop at the platform in Ardmore, Brooks thrust open a door and leaped onto the decking, running to keep from falling. Josef slumped to the floor of the car.

EPILOGUE

Ray didn't have all his strength back, but he was definitely feeling better than anyone could have predicted. He didn't exactly have a bounce in his step as he walked south to the light, where he would cross to the west side of the avenue. He inhaled the air of freedom. He had survived the threats of being torpedoed by a Nazi submarine, and he would not be slogging through the snows of Europe as a foot soldier when the Allied armies began to push toward Berlin—the Americans and British from the west and Stalin's Red Army from the east. Would he have a long life? Probably not. But recalling that the Army doctor had hinted that he might not live long enough to make the trip from Corpus Christi to Austin, Ray could not deny that his life was definitely on the upswing. When he reached the colorfully decorated windows of Scarborough's department store, Ray realized he was slowing down. It was time to cross the street and head back, even though Ray was no more certain about his future than he had been when he had concluded that a walk was just what he needed to help him make a plan for the rest of his life.

Today was a very good day, and Ray was still smiling when he opened the door of the Longhorn. Still smiling perhaps, but he was winded, and he needed to sit down. Ray noticed that Myrtle was smiling as well—smiling so big that she was about to burst. She was positively glowing.

"You have a visitor," she announced, "and she's a looker, too!" Myrtle winked at Ray, who followed her eyes as she turned her head and looked directly at a booth in the back corner of the dining room. The mystery woman seated and waiting with a cup of coffee and glass of ice water spread in front of her was very attractive in a unique sort of way. Her hair was somewhere close to auburn. She wore glasses that resembled the style his mother favored. Her face was regal. There was no other way Ray could describe it. The only makeup Ray could detect was a trace of flesh toned lipstick. She smiled broadly, clearly recognizing Ray, who was certain that he did not know her at all.

As Ray began walking toward her table, he realized that she looked like a much younger version of his mother. But there was one marked difference that became apparent as she began to stand in anticipation of Ray's arrival. This young lady, likely close to Ray's age, was very tall, much taller than his mother, and probably very close to Ray's height, five feet eleven. She was stunning. As Ray reached her booth, she extended her hand, and Ray took it.

"I am your cousin," she told him. "My name is Thelma Alsobrook, and your mother, my Aunt Ada, is my very favorite relative. I have only seen her in person twice in my life—once as a very small girl, and this past week when I visited her at your home in Telegraph, a beautiful place."

Cousin? That's what she'd said. And she did look very much like his mother. Her smile was warm, and much like Ada's. There was a glow to this young woman that mesmerized Ray. He knew he had lots of cousins, but he had only met a few and had paid little attention to any of them.

"Aunt Ada and I have become close friends through our letters. We have written to one another at least twice a month since right after I started school, so I have heard a whole lot about you through the years. And I just saw a number of photographs of you, when I stayed at your home. So that's why I recognized you right away." Thelma continued to talk. At some point she had released his hand and returned to her seat. Ray had sat in the booth opposite from his cousin. A cup of coffee and a glass of ice water had just been placed in front of him by Natalie, one of the regular waitresses.

"Can we offer you something to eat?" Ray asked as Natalie stood poised with a pad and pencil. Ray suddenly realized that these were the first words he had spoken to Thelma.

"Oh, I don't think so," she answered. "I've got to get back to my train. The stop is just an hour, but Aunt Ada will be so delighted to hear that I actually got to meet you."

Ray looked at Natalie. "I'll have them box up a BLT and a slice of apple pie for the train, then," Natalie suggested. Ray nodded, and the waitress headed for the service window with the order.

"Wow, you look a lot more like your father than I had anticipated. I think your brother Ralph looks a lot like my father, but you definitely favor Uncle Walter, though you're a bit taller." Thelma paused for a moment, smiled, then explained. "I usually don't rattle on like this. Actually, I don't talk much at all. I'm a school librarian, but I am excited to meet you and to be able to tell Aunt Ada how well you look."

Ray was confused. He knew that most of his father's siblings had settled in Fort Worth, even though they were all from New Mexico. But he knew almost nothing about his mother's family. He knew she had grown up on a farm along the Pedernales River, and Ray vaguely recalled that Ralph had stayed with an uncle in St. Louis. Perhaps that uncle was related to his mother.

"So you're from St. Louis, maybe? And that's where you're going?" he asked.

Thelma laughed a little. "Well, sort of," she said. "I grew up in St. Louis, and I went to the St. Louis Normal School. That's where I studied to be a teacher and a school librarian. I have a younger brother named Sid, and he met and married a girl from Minden, Louisiana, not too far from Shreveport. I know you used to work in the oil fields, so I am guessing you know where Shreveport is?" Thelma paused and Ray nodded.

"Well, only about a year after they got married, my sister-in-law wrote saying that her aunt was retiring as the school librarian, and her aunt would recommend me for the job in Minden. So that's where I am now."

The box lunch arrived, and Thelma began searching through her purse. "No, the meal is on the house. If you're Ray's cousin, then you're Brooks' cousin, too. And he runs the Longhorn when he's not off serving in the Army. So Miss Myrtle said you were our guest," Natalie concluded.

Thelma looked at Ray. He nodded, so she snapped her purse closed. "Thank you so much. I really appreciate this," Thelma said to Natalie and nodded to Ray, who smiled and nodded again.

"Oh I hate to just rush into all this, especially with you barely knowing who I am, if at all. But honestly, your mother sent me to see you, and told me I must tell you some things, if I got to see you. So, I just have to blurt them right out, because I promised."

"I understand," Ray agreed, still totally baffled by what was going on.

"As I said, your mother and I write to each other about everything, and I do mean everything. So when you got so sick, Aunt Ada was just worried to death that you were going to die. It nearly killed her. I'm sorry to say it that way, but that's absolutely true.

"Now she's never said a word to me about your brother Glenn getting killed, but my Dad told me all about it. And over the years, when your brother Ralph got in all that trouble during prohibition, that again was something that nearly killed your mother. Sometimes I saw ink smears on the letters, which I felt must have been caused by her tears."

Ray took in a quick breath, attempting to control his own emotions. It was becoming clear where this conversation was heading. It was bad medicine, and it was going to be painful, but Ray absolutely knew that he had to listen. He had done these things to his mother, and he had to sit and take it. Thoughts raced through his mind, and he was fighting a big distraction. The messenger his mother had sent to him was stunningly beautiful, a total stranger, a cousin he had never heard of; and the whole thing was going to be worse because this beautiful woman looked so much like Ada must have when she had been young.

"And there was your first disappearance riding a freight train, and the second, and Brooks getting hurt and not being able to play football ever again. And then there was the horrible disappointment with Maryon marrying that philanderer. That broke Aunt Ada's heart, but she said it almost killed Uncle Walter. He just couldn't stand it. And the business with Jimmie—that seems to never stop. And her being in the Army now. The worry just never ends for your folks." Thelma took a breath.

"I'm sorry. I'm making a mess of this. But your mother said you needed to know what you were doing to the people who love you so much and just looking at you I can see why they do. You're just gorgeous! Oh, God! I just said that out loud, and I didn't mean to, but it's true.

"And Aunt Ada says that you might be the smartest of all the kids, and I can see why she would say that, too. She says all of you seem like maybe you're too smart for your own good. And she can't figure out why people so smart keep doing such stupid things. And she thinks you don't know that she knew about all the fighting and drinking you did while you were working in the oil fields and on that pipeline down on the coast somewhere. But she knew. She heard your father talking on the phone to people at the jails and judges and sheriffs. And she said that finally she made your sister Edythe and Cousin Jimmie tell her every bit of it.

"And she doesn't know why you're not dead, but she's so glad you're not. And the real thing she wants me to tell you is how much she loves you, and you have to promise me that you won't throw away this last chance at life. She just loves you too much. Just too much, and I see why. Promise me!" Thelma said as she stood, forcing back tears.

"I promise," Ray managed, his voice faint and cracking when he spoke. Ray was slightly unsteady as he rose from his seat. Neither of them was crying, but they were so close.

Just as Ray reached his feet, his cousin stepped toward him and grabbed him tightly around the neck with a strong left arm. With her right hand on his left cheek, Thelma kissed Ray with more intensity than any woman ever had. Her lips did not open, nor did Ray dare open his mouth. But he had never been kissed like that in his whole life.

"You're gorgeous," she said a second time, "but I'm going to miss my train."

"No you're not, hon," Myrtle said, riding to the rescue. "Get that box, please Natalie?" she added while guiding Thelma toward the door. Myrtle had Ray's cousin by the elbow as she thrust open the glass door. Three steps and Miss Alsobrook felt herself being helped into the backseat of a taxi. Natalie put the box lunch in her lap. Myrtle slapped a five-dollar bill into the cabbie's hand. Natalie closed the door, and the well-practiced cab driver took off for the Missouri Pacific Depot.

There had been only a few customers in the cafe to witness Ray and Thelma's encounter. With all of them following his cousin's departure, Ray took advantage of the distraction to make his own exit upstairs to Brooks' room above the restaurant. Ray looked out the dirty window in time to see the cab taking Thelma to the train, as it made a right turn onto Eleventh Street. he stared at the Capitol for a moment, then sat in the threadbare old chair that both Oakley brothers used as a reading perch. Everything in his mother's message that had poured out of Thelma was true. And for the first time, Ray had some context in which to place his own reckless behavior into a full picture of how his siblings, Glenn, Ralph, Brooks, Maryon and Jimmie had brought so much pain and anguish to their parents, especially Ada.

It had taken three full sets of loud knocks to finally rouse Ray, who was ordinarily a light sleeper. He only remembered sitting in the chair, replaying the meeting with Thelma. He must have fallen asleep in the chair and somehow found his way onto the bed at some point, because that's where he was as the pounding on the door continued. "Mr. Ray, it's Natalie," he heard. "We need your help downstairs."

Ray felt around for his glasses, slipped them on, then immediately removed them so he could rub sleep from his eyes. He stood, prepared to reach for his bathrobe before realizing that he was still completely dressed. Even his shoes were still on. The light from Congress Avenue was enough to illuminate the door, where Ray headed, once he had stood. "What are you doing here?" he asked Natalie. "It must be after midnight," Ray guessed.

"I had to come back to relieve Myrtle. Pearl didn't show. But right now, Rudy could really use your help." Ray had begun following Natalie down the steps. As the pair reached the bottom of the stairs and moved into the dining room, Ray saw the problem at once. He reached under the counter for the big Louisville Slugger kept there for these situations. Three big drunks, two of them ex-cons that Ray recognized as regulars to the Longhorn, had the cook, Rudy Flores, backed into a corner adjacent to the booth where he had sat with his cousin something like eight hours earlier. Without a word, Ray stepped forward and collapsed the biggest of the drunks, a convicted killer called Blondie with a mighty blow to the back of the convict's knees. Ray quickly followed with a stomp into Blondie's crotch to make sure he would stay down.

Rudy needed no encouragement. He smacked the second con, a shorter, but very muscular man who went by Curly, against the side of his face with a medium sized iron skillet he had been holding poised in his left hand. Rudy turned and prepared to lurch at the third drunk with an eight-inch butcher knife Rudy gripped tightly in his right hand. Ray held the barrel of the Louisville Slugger just above Rudy's nose, shielding the cook's eyes so that he temporarily lost line of sight with the last drunk standing. Ray scowled at the final attacker and growled one word, "Run!"

The now sobered up drunk took a single step back, turned and took off for the door. Ray gripped the Louisville Slugger mid-barrel like a football and hurled a perfect spiral that struck the fleeing man right between the shoulder blades. The blow sent the man sprawling through the open door. He skidded across the sidewalk on his belly, losing most of the skin on his forehead and all of the skin on his nose. In a second, he was back on his feet and running for his life down the sidewalk.

Rudy glared at Ray, fuming because his boss' brother had stopped him from sticking the drunk with his butcher knife. "Splash some water on your face and cool off. Stabbing that guy wasn't worth a trip to the penitentiary," Ray told the cook. "I've got to go to the bathroom. When you're ready, would you mind fixing me some scrambled eggs and chili, Rudy?"

"Natalie, could you find Big Swede and ask him to get those two drunks out of here. And if he decides not to violate their paroles, could you have Swede tell them that they're not to come back in here until each one of them has apologized to Rudy and given him a hundred dollars each?" Natalie smiled. Clearly Ray was like his older brother in many ways. And certainly that was true when it came to knowing his way around a bar fight.

When Ray came out of the washroom, his eggs were sitting on the counter next to the cash register. He chuckled, knowing that Rudy would be angry for days. Ray wondered whether Rudy had spit in his eggs, or worse. Just as he was sopping up the last of the chili with his third biscuit, the phone rang. The call lasted less than fifteen seconds. "Police dispatcher," Natalie said. "Big Swede's on his way. He just wrapped up a homicide on Chacon Street. Anything else you want me to tell him?"

"That should do," Ray answered as he rose and walked around to the other side of the lunch counter. He located two paper cups, filled them with coffee and put lids on them. Natalie knew that Ray wanted to be gone before the giant policeman arrived. He waited by the alley door until he heard the door slam on the squad car out front, then slipped out the back, turned left and walked through the alley toward Eleventh Street. He crossed over to the Capitol Grounds, walking under the giant elms until he found a bench that the birds had not completely fouled about halfway between the street and the steps of the building. Ray took a sip of his first coffee and recalled the summary of his conversation with Thelma that he had created in his memory the night before as he sat in Brooks' room. So what exactly had Ray's mother intended for him to do? He boiled it down to two things he thought he could live with: stay alive and use his intelligence.

Ray was in fact grateful to be alive, and the encounter with his cousin Thelma and that kiss. He had to admit that this incredible young lady had given him insight into a whole world that he had never considered before, even for a second. Not that he could run off to Louisiana and marry his own cousin, but still.

Ray allowed himself to pause on that thought. She had shown him that there was a world that didn't require him to stay drunk and fight most of the time. Would he stop drinking? That seemed to be what at least two doctors were suggesting. Married? Not to Thelma, of course, but could he actually marry someone who taught school or was a nurse in a hospital or a secretary in an office? Could he really have that kind of life? After all, he had a certificate from a business school that said he was a bookkeeper. Could he go back to that? There was no rule that said an office had to be in a shack in an oil camp or somewhere that drunken brawlers like he had been himself worked. Bookkeepers were needed in all kinds of businesses—even in government offices and schools. Wouldn't that be something, him getting a job in an office? Ray knew that would certainly make his mother proud.

He had heard jobs were plentiful. He had been told he could work at the Longhorn for as long as he needed or wished. He could go back to Telegraph, knowing full well that his father would find him work there, or get him a job at the railroad. He was standing less than a mile from the University of Texas, and he was still young. He could walk over, sign up, and learn to be anything he wished. Walter would pay. Or he could work his way through at the Longhorn the way his brother had.

What was next for Ray Oakley? Perhaps someone knew, but Ray had no idea.

ABOUT THE AUTHOR

Phil Oakley is a writer, educator, filmmaker, journalist and executive. He is the author of eight novels. He began working on his first one in the spring of 1964, while a freshman at The University of Texas at Austin. That book finally reached publication fifty years later in 2014. In addition to writing, Phil currently works as a paraprofessional educator at Kennedale High School.

Previously, he served as Director of the Louisiana Film Commission, was a regional executive of The Walt Disney Company, supervising coverage for ABC News in the south-

Photo by Brooks Oakley

western United States and Latin America. He also was an editor/producer for *The Dallas Morning News*. As a journalist, Phil won national awards from Columbia University, the Radio-Television News Directors' Association and a National Headliners Award. He covered presidents and presidential campaigns, beginning with Lyndon Johnson and extending through the terms of George W. Bush. Phil was born in Austin during the last days of World War II. He lives in Arlington, Texas with his wife, the former Nancy Matens of Baton Rouge. Both are graduates of Louisiana State University. They have two sons and one granddaughter.

THE OAKLEYS WILL RETURN

Look for the next installments in the series:
Longhorn
Coming soon from

We publish the stories you've been waiting to read

Check out our other titles at StoneyCreekPublishing.com.

For author book signings, speaking engagements, or other events, please contact us at info@stoneycreekpublishing.com

www.ingramcontent.com/pod-product-compliance
Lightning Source LLC
Jackson TN
JSHW080815260225
79356JS00004BA/39